ICE
COLD
HELL

To
David R Fleiger

12-08-2018

Best Wishes

Joe

ICE
COLD
HELL

JOE WEALL

BROWN
DOG
BOOKS

Published under licence by Brown Dog Books and
The Self-Publishing Partnership, 7 Green Park Station, Bath BA1 1JB

www.selfpublishingpartnership.co.uk

ISBN printed book: 978-1-78545-074-7
ISBN e-book: 978-1-78545-075-4

Cover design by Kevin Rylands
Internal design by Tim Jollands

Printed and bound by CPI Group (UK) Ltd, Croydon CR0 4YY

To you it looks like a log cabin. To me it looks like Heaven, Utopia, and Salvation; I only hope I am not imagining it and it is really there.

Perhaps I should explain.

It started two weeks ago when I lost my horse. He broke a leg after falling, when he was running in deep snow on my way back to the cabin. I tried to stick to the trail the best I could, but it was very difficult with two or so feet of snow on it.

The snow had come overnight when I was asleep. I should have taken more notice of where I had come from, and not have been dreaming so much. I did have a compass but never looked at it once. I am now paying the price.

I had come to Canada to work; it was my first time here, and I had just come from the Sahara where I worked as a welding inspector.

When I left the Sahara it was 110 degrees. All I'd worn when I was there was a tee shirt and shorts, and some days that was too much.

Arriving in Canada two weeks later it was quite chilly; just about freezing point in fact. I think I was the one who really felt it most. Coming from where I had, this was a new experience for me.

I had worked in the Arab countries for the last six or seven years, where it is hot most of the time. Here in Canada at this time of year it is a lot different from what I was used to. It was cold, but clean, crisp, sunny, clear and dry, not like the winters back in Britain; wet and miserable.

I was to start work on the following day on an oil refinery, welding pipes in the open air.

Before going to work the next morning, I had put on two pairs of jeans, a couple of sweaters and a big coat and I was still cold when I was working.

At lunch time I said to a local, 'I don't think I will be here long.'

'Why?' he asked.

'I'm bloody freezing that's why. I have just come from Algeria where it is nice and warm at the moment; nothing like this.'

'What will you do when winter comes?' he remarked.

'Are you joking? You mean to say this is not winter?'

'No,' he said. 'There is a lot worse to come. Believe me this is quite mild for this time of year.'

'Quite mild, that's done it; I am definitely off by the weekend.'

'Don't be silly. When you have finished work tonight go over to Woolco and buy some good winter clothing. I will meet you there if you like. Let's say half past eight.'

'Yes, you are on. That's if I am not an ice lollipop by then and I am still alive.'

After work I went back to the chalet, had a hot shower and made my way to the canteen. There was curry on the menu, so that's what I had. I was feeling a lot warmer now.

After my dinner I crossed the road to Woolco. Sure enough, the local was there having coffee at a small diner.

'Hi,' he said. 'How are you feeling now?'

'A damn sight warmer than I was at work.'

'Come on, let's get you rigged out then.'

The boots he recommended had a half inch felt lining. They felt very big to me, but also very warm. When I walked in them I felt like Frankenstein.

Some padded work pants, jacket, some thermal underwear and socks; that should do the trick, hopefully. The funny thing is they were not that expensive. There is no reason to be cold out here. I was looking forward to wearing these for work tomorrow. It should be a lot easier and warmer working,

After we had finished the shopping, he asked me if I would like a beer with him at George's tavern down the town.

'Certainly. I will buy you a few beers, it's the least I can do. By the way what is your name?'

'Homer.'

'Homer?'

'Homer D. Byrd.'

'Are you from around here, Homer?'

'Hell no! I am from the good old United States of America.'

'I thought you were a local. I have not been listening to your accent very closely. Come to think of it, I have been too bloody cold to notice anything, let alone accents. What part of the States?' I asked him.

'Mobile, Alabama,' he replied.

'Christ, you are a long way from home, is there no work down there?'

'Not a lot at the moment, so I thought I would give this a try.'

'How long have you been here?' I asked?

'Going on seven months now.'

We walked back to the camp and I dumped my shopping off, then we got a taxi into town.

George's tavern wasn't the classiest place I have been in. It was dark and dingy, but it was full, and people were singing and enjoying themselves. Homer seemed to know quite a lot of the men in there. We sat down and a waiter with an old fashioned white apron wrapped around his big fat waist, just like in the gangster films, came over to take our order.

'What would you like, Homer?' I asked.

'You had better make it four beers each.'

'Four! Are you thirsty or something?'

'Not particularly. It is best this way, to order when there are so many people in, it saves you waiting.' When we were on the third drink, in came three big Mounties. One stood at the front door, one stood halfway and the third went looking around for someone; the first two had their truncheons drawn, it was fascinating to watch. Knowing my luck he will pick me out, and I have just got here.

While he was looking round, everything went quiet.

When he found who he was looking for he pulled out his revolver and pointed it at the man's head and said, 'Can we have a word with you?'

The man could hardly say no could he?

After they left, everything got back to normal very quickly.

I asked Homer, 'Is that a common practice around here? The police back home do not even carry guns.'

'Yes, if they want you, they do not mess about.'

I finished my four beers, and said to Homer, 'Thanks for your help, I will see you tomorrow at work.'

'Hang on, I have not got you a drink,' he said.

'There is no need, I have enjoyed the ones I have had; thanks and goodnight.'

I left before he or his mates insisted I have more.

At work next day, it was as I expected and I was a lot warmer. I talked all day of the happenings of the night before in George's tavern, but no one else seemed impressed about it at all.

The first week seemed to flash past; I have changed my mind, I will be staying now.

I soon fell in love with Canada, the people, the land and their customs. I became friendly quite quickly with most of my workmates, but that's the sort of man I am.

On the odd night I would have a drink with Homer and some of the locals with whom I was working. Homer was a right old character. I found out later the old bugger was sixty-eight years old, and he was as straight as a die. They were all right, down to earth, no frills. What you see is what you get.

One or two of the locals had log cabins up in the woods. (When they say woods, they mean two or three hundred square miles of forest.)

I liked the idea of being out in the wilds like that and said to myself, one day I would give it a try. You know what I mean, we have all seen it at the cinema,

That's what I wanted to try, go north up into the wilds, with a horse, and carry all my supplies with me. (It was just a dream.)

I was from a small northern town in England called Barrow-in-Furness. It was in Lancashire, now Cumbria.

I never ever thought that one day, the opportunity would

present itself. But now I am here in Canada, talking to these men who have cabins in the wilds; there may be a chance of fulfilling that dream. If I am lucky enough, who knows, I think I would like to give it a go.

I had travelled quite a lot with my job and enjoyed most of it. Welding, welding inspecting and supervising. I had been to Iran, Iraq, Algeria, Qatar and all around Europe, but this was a new experience for me. When this job finishes, which by the way was in St John, New Brunswick, maybe I could go with one of the locals to his cabin and live my dream.

I was telling Mike Butler about my dream of going up north, and staying in a log cabin. We had worked together recruiting men for this job, from back home.

He asked me if I would like to use his log cabin.

'Are you joking, Mike?'

'No, I normally use it myself two or three times a year but I have a new contract to set up, so as I will not be using it this winter. Would you like to go and check it out for me?'

This was my chance to fulfil that dream.

'Where is it, Mike?' I asked.

'It's near Lake Mistassini in Quebec.'

'Where the hell is that? And how would I get there?'

'It's only about six hundred miles north west of here.'

'Only,' I gulped.

Mike said that he normally goes in his four wheel drive to within forty miles of the cabin.

Then he does the rest by skidoo; that's if there is enough snow. If not, he rents a couple of horses, one mount and one pack horse, and that takes about two, maybe three days to get to the cabin.

'You can use them if you go.'

'Use what?' I asked.

'The four wheeler and skidoo,' he answered.

Well at first I was not too sure. It is always the same, the chance pops up and you tend to have second thoughts. I knew very little about surviving in the wilds of Canada or anywhere else for that matter. I had heard a lot of talk of how some people did go out into the wilds and were never heard of again, but the pull was too much for me to resist. I would get some books out of the library and read up on how to get through the worst just in case the winter did get bad. I would talk to as many locals as possible, to those who I know have cabins.

Mike had told me it can get to twenty, maybe forty degrees below freezing with the wind chill factor and several feet of snow. He said the main thing was if you get caught out when the weather worsens; keep out of the wind if it gets up.

'But I will tell you now,' he said. 'No book can tell you how it's going to be. Mother Nature does not read books and, just like a woman, does what she likes, when she likes, sometimes without rhyme or reason.

Well, do I take his offer up or do I go home, that was the question? If I go home it will be to no job and because it is winter it may be some weeks before I get one. If I should want to take this adventure some other time in the future it would cost me a small fortune. Whereas now I have been offered a free vehicle and a log cabin for as long as I like.

I asked Mike, 'When do you think I should go?'

'It would take you about a week to get things together,' said Mike. 'I will help you all I can. First I will get the four wheeler serviced, and help you order some supplies, maps and so on.

Can you use a rifle?'

'Yes, of course I can. What sort you are talking about?'

'Oh,' he casually said, 'a .308 or a Winchester 30-06.'

'I have fired a .22,' I said, thinking that was okay.

He never laughed but a broad smile came on his face. It was a big smile. He was a big lad, 6'1" and about sixteen stone (250 pounds) and not an ounce of fat?

'No,' he said. 'I mean a rifle.'

'Okay Mike. Is there any chance of you taking me to a shooting range and showing me what you mean?'

Mike asked, 'Are you doing anything on Saturday morning?

'No. What do you have in mind?'

'I could take you to the shooting range for a couple of hours, if that's okay with you,' he suggested.

'Right,' I said. 'I am game for anything, I think I will enjoy that.'

This he did and off to the range we went. I could not wait to see these rifles.

It was about 8.30 a.m. when we got to the shooting range and we had the place to ourselves. He unpacked the guns, they looked awesome. They were magnificent things to look at. To think this beautiful workmanship was designed just to kill. Nothing like the .22 I had fired.

'Right,' he said. 'Which do you want to try first?'

'You go first,' I said, 'and let me see how they go.'

He loaded the 30.06 Winchester, which worked just like the ones the cowboys use. He took aim and fired. The noise was deafening and even big Mike was knocked back a little.

'Christ,' I said, 'what do you use that for?'

I don't think he heard me.

'Right! Now it's your turn,' he said.

'I think I will try the other one, if you don't mind.'

'Certainly. Would you like to load it yourself?'

'Yes, that's a good idea. It might just give me the feel of it.'

The magazine held five bullets and it was a bolt action.

So now it's loaded ready for firing.

'Go ahead,' said Mike. 'Aim for that target over there, keep the gun tight to your shoulder and squeeze the trigger gently.'

This I did.

'I now know why you were smiling, you big berk.' The recoil of the gun nearly put me on my arse, not to mention hurting my bloody shoulder.'

'Well,' said Mike. 'I have brought plenty of ammo and we have a couple of hours, so let's start again.'

Two hours later I was quite a crack shot, even Mike was impressed. I was also very pleased with my progress in such a short time.

I asked him what the .308 is used for.

'That's the one you should take,' he said. 'It's zeroed in at 200 metres. You would use it for deer, wolf and bears.'

'Wolves and bears,' I said. 'Are you kidding me?'

'No, I am not. That's why I wanted you to learn how to use one before you go to the cabin.

You should be okay. You may have to shoot deer for food; that's if you go by horse as that way you are limited to what you can carry. If any wolves or bears come near, fire a shot into the air and the noise of the shot usually frightens them away; that is if they are not too hungry.' He smiled.

'Behave yourself, Mike! You are putting me off going now.'

'As I said before, you will be okay.'

Well if he has the confidence in me, then I should have also; that's what I said to myself, fingers crossed.

I had a quiet day on Sunday just reading and thinking all the time about my trip. Monday afternoon things are moving fast now, I don't have a lot of time to worry about anything, I have to see about supplies, etc.

The next thing I know I'm driving along the trans-Canada highway in Mike's four wheeler with a skidoo in the back, and what seemed far too many supplies. There was just about everything.

Mike had made up the list and before I set off he had sat and talked to me nearly all night. After which, I felt I knew something about surviving; well that's how I felt. He had phoned the farmer/garage owner and told him about me coming. I was to ask for a Joe Weall.

When I got to the place, he would see to my skidoo, or the horses, whichever I was to use.

Before I had left, Mike had given me a bottle of Nuffie screech. "Have a little nip of that at night, before you go to bed, it will help you sleep," he had said.

I accepted his gift but I never needed help sleeping, I am an expert in the art of sleeping; it came naturally. If anything I could do with something to keep me awake.

I was about two and half hours into my journey when it dawned upon me, I had never ridden a horse or ever been on a skidoo. With all the excitement I had never given it a thought until now. Oh well, it is too late to worry about that now, and I will just have to learn the hard way.

There can't be much to riding a horse, little kids do it don't they? And a skidoo must be like riding a motorbike. Then again, I have never ridden a motorbike.

I can see there is going to be some fun ahead.

I was not prepared as much as I thought I was and I had a funny feeling that I was going off half cocked. I was passing through Grand Falls now, it looked like a tourist place, and I would like to spend a couple of hours here on the way back.

First, I had to get to Chibougamau in Quebec, and that was just the first step. To get there I had to pass through Edmondson and on to Rivière-du-Loup from where I cross the St Lawrence River heading for Chicoutimi, passing Lake St John. Then onto Dolbeau.

I have noticed on my drive from St John the trees seemed to go on and on; this was a great feature of my journey, they were never ending.

I kept driving until I got to Rivière-du-Loup when I realised how tired I was, so it was the nearest motel for me.

After booking into the motel I had a nice meal and then it was off to bed. I did not take much rocking and I had a good night's sleep.

Next morning, up bright and early for a plate of pancakes with a lot of maple syrup and a mug of sweet coffee. Then I filled up the four wheel drive, bought some cans of pop and snacks ready for crossing the St Lawrence over to St Simeon. I really feel I am on the way now.

After crossing the St Lawrence River I find I have to speak more and more French. This was not much of a problem, as I had learnt some French in Algeria. I did once have a bungalow in Brittany.

I'm in no rush, so it will be another overnight stay, because I realised I did too much yesterday and it nearly spoilt my journey, which is the last thing I want to do. Looking at the map, I thought I would stop somewhere between Chicoutimi and Chibougamau; that's if there is anything between.

But for now I'm going to enjoy the trip to the cabin.

Looking at the map again, I chose Dolbeau. I will stop off there, I reckon it's only about 85 to maybe 110 miles. I know it's not far, but as I said I did too much the first day and got over tired. I did not enjoy that too much, so it's slower from now on. Arriving at Chicoutimi it was about 3.00 p.m. It was still quite sunny and pleasant so I thought, well I would find a motel, park up and have a walk around, work up a bit of an appetite then take a little nap, after which I may even have a couple of beers.

There was not much to see, but I enjoyed the walk and with the sun sinking it was turning just a little cold now; so it's a meal, then a nap. When I woke up I felt really good. No wonder. Looking at the clock it was 7.45 p.m. So I had slept for over two hours.

After taking a shower, which was so refreshing, I am ready for a few beers and see what the nightlife is like around here. Not much I bet.

Well, I am in the pub now which is not far from the motel. On the way in you have to go through swing doors into the pub, which had a wooden floor and not much else. Oh, it did have a bar.

There were six or seven people inside already. Three or four people followed me in, some of them looked like cowboys and the others like lumberjacks, and it looked like a scene out of *Blazing Saddles*.

'What will you have, buddy?' asked the barman.

'I don't suppose you have a pint of Tetley bitter?'

He looked at me for a moment and said, 'We have light beer or you could have a light beer.'

'You had best give me a light beer,' I replied.

Well, as I said earlier, I am a friendly person at the best of time, but with some beer in me I love the world.

I bought some beers for a couple of the locals whom I got taking to, and everybody in the place wanted to talk to me; it must be because of my accent. That was okay but they also got me a beer. Not being a drinking man it was getting to me very quickly and they asked me about a thousand questions.

Where was I from? Where was I going to? And why was I going to the log cabin at this time of the year? You should come back in the summer, it is very nice around here. Which part of England did I live in and so on?

Well, we told a few jokes and in general, I had a good night.

It's 10.45 p.m. now and the beer is really getting to me, so I shook hands with everyone and said goodnight in English and in French so as not to offend anyone.

They were still asking me questions as I was on my way out of the door.

The motel room was lovely and warm. Boy did that feel nice. I hung my clothes up on the floor and fell into bed.

Next morning when I awoke, much to my surprise I felt quite good. All I needed now was a good English breakfast with everything, eggs, bacon, beans, toast and anything else they can get on the plate. Now that would set me up for the day. The waitress asked would I like some home fries.

'What are they?' I enquired.

'Boiled potatoes, sliced and fried,' she said.

Sounds good to me; they even had brown HP sauce.

I don't know why but I always feel that I could eat a horse after being on the beer the night before.

I shouldn't say that, I may have to before I get back.

Most of, if not all my mates can't even look at food, never mind eat any after a good night out, and certainly not as much as I do.

Boy, that was good. I am ready for anything.

It's another sunny morning but I can feel it getting colder. The ice on the roadside pools seems to be a lot thicker. Still, that will not stop me getting there, once again nice and slow so I can enjoy the drive.

Every day I say to myself what a fantastic country this is, and I often wonder if the Canadians know just what they have.

Well, I am heading for Chibougamau and will soon know if it is to be skidoo or the horses. Judging by the weather it looks like the horses.

I was hoping to go by skidoo. I think it would be a lot easier and faster but there is no turning back now. Maybe it's for the best; I can pretend to be a cowboy. I think I'll be Cheyenne Bodie. (Well it's my dream.)

I should be in Chibougamau sometime today. Again, I think I will stay overnight. I am in no hurry and will get an early start in the morning, then I can do a whole day on the road and get a few miles in.

I hope the horses I get are friendly, the last thing I want is to be struggling with them. I know it is going to be too far to walk, so we will have to get along somehow.

On my approach to Chibougamau I stopped and asked for directions from someone who looked like a native of the area. He had a red windswept face, with wrinkles and looked about 120 years old, but I guess he is only around 30.

'Please can you tell me how to get to Joe Weall's garage?' I asked.

Well, he started to speak to me but I have no idea in what language he was speaking. There was a bit of French and I think some Eskimo and the odd word of English.

Trust me! I thought. I always pick them.

I wrote the name down for him to look at.

He gave a grunt and pointed down the road, then held up three fingers. Did that mean three miles, three kilometres or three days? I just didn't know.

Anyway I thanked him as well as I could and drove on. It turned out to be three miles.

I found the place easy enough, it was on the main road just as I got into town. I thought this was a bit lucky as the town seemed to be of a fair size.

I pulled up alongside the garage. I thought, overall, that was a nice drive and I have enjoyed the trip so far, let's hope it all goes as well from now on.

'Bonjour, monsieur.'

'Bonjour,' I said. 'Parlez-vous anglais.'

'Oui,' he said. 'What I can do for you?'

Well, it was nearly English.

'I am Mike Butler's friend. Did he let you know I was coming? I will be using his cabin for a couple of weeks.'

'Oh, oui, oui,' he said, slipping back into French for a moment; he smiled broadly.

I thought he was going to hug me.

But he shook my hand and said, 'You are from the old country, Mike did not say. I thought you would be a Canadian. My parents were English. They were from Bolton, Lancashire,' he said very proudly. 'Do you know of it?'

'Yes, I live about one and a half hours' drive north west from there,' I replied.

He was still shaking my hand about three minutes later. He had big hands, very big.

When the feeling returned to my hand I asked, 'What would be the best way to get to Mike's cabin?'

He thought for a little while, looking up at the sky, and around at the same time and said, 'You should leave it for four or five days then you can go by skidoo, otherwise it will be the horse.'

How does he know there will be enough snow in four or five days' time just by looking around. I did not want to stay in town that long not knowing anyone, so I told him I would like to set out tomorrow.

'That's up to you,' he said. 'What would you like to do today?'

'Can we get the horses ready?' I asked.

'That will not take long,' came the reply. 'Come out back. I will show you which two I will pick out for you.'

The back of the garage looked out on to what looked like a very big farm.

He showed me two which I thought were nice horses, but to me they looked bloody big things.

'Have you no smaller?' I asked.

'These are small.' he replied.

'How is their temperament?' I asked.

Joe seemed to know that this was my first time around horses.

'Oh, you will have no trouble from these two, they know the routine backwards. They will look after you. Leave your car here, book into the motel across the road and tell Nadine, Joe sent you. She will give you the room a bit cheaper.'

'What time will you be taking supper?' Joe asked. (That's teatime to me.)

'Around six to six thirty,' I replied.

'Go to the Arc-en-Ciel along Maple St, it's about five minute walk on the right. I will join you and we can talk better.'

'Okay, that sounds good to me. See you there.'

I got a few things out of the car and walked over the road to the motel which was almost opposite. When I walked in the door the heat hit me in the face; they always have it far too high over here in winter.

I rang the bell on the counter and a woman came from out of an office. She was very attractive with a lovely figure, aged about 37, with long black raven hair, down to her hips like an Indian squaw you see in films, but much more beautiful in real life.

She obviously looks after herself, I thought.

'Bonjour, madam.'

'Bonjour, monsieur.'

'Joe sent me over. He said you would have a room for me.'

'You are English!' she said.

'Yes, that's right,' I replied.

She asked, 'How long will you be staying?'

'Just the one night.' And then quick as a flash, 'Two, if you will have dinner with me tomorrow night.'

Much to my surprise she said, 'I would like that very much.'

'Okay then, perhaps you can recommend somewhere nice to eat.'

'Yes,' she said 'the Arc-en-Ciel. It is a very nice restaurant with a lounge bar.'

'That's where I am having a drink tonight with Joe. I will see you in the morning and make arrangements then. Unless you would like to join us tonight?

'No thank you. I must work tonight but not tomorrow,' she replied.

'Okay, no problem,' I said.

She gave me the key to my room and directed me. I put my bag inside and went straight back to Joe's.

I told him I would be staying an extra night.

'Pourquoi?' he asked.

When I told him why, he said, 'You are a fast worker, there's a few in this town who would like half a chance.'

'Anyway,' I said, 'it's for the best. It gives me another day to learn something about the horses and you can show me about putting the saddle on, and everything else.

I went back to my room feeling very pleased with myself.

I dozed until five thirty, I then got up and had a shower and a shave. When I say a shave, I mean thirty seconds with an electric razor. I'm luckier than most other men, no wet shaving for me as I only have a very light growth. I got dressed and wandered down to the restaurant. I found the place easy enough. On the way there, I noticed how very cold it was.

Walking into the foyer, the bar was on the right and the restaurant on the left. It was a very nice place; again the heat hit me when I walked in.

'Limey. In here,' came a French accent from the bar.

'Bonsoir,' I said. 'You okay, oui?'

'Oui, merci,' he replied. 'What do you want to drink?'

'What is that you are drinking?' I asked.

'Chardonnay,' he said.

'When are we having something to eat?Later?' I enquired.

'Oui. Oui,' Joe said.

'In that case, I will have the same as you.

Can I buy a bottle for us? And perhaps we can have a talk before we have had too much wine.'

'Yes, let us sit at a table and you can ask me all the questions you want about the horses and staying at the cabin.'

I asked him about the cabin, the area, and things to watch out for and so on.

He emphasised about keeping an eye on the weather as it will snow within the next week. And any wild life I came across, just be careful and alert at all times.

When the third bottle came, we were talking gibberish. The more wine I had, the more French I spoke. The more Joe had, the more English he spoke (I think).

It reminded me of the time I was working in Algeria.

Two new welders were on their way out to Algeria and

they met in Paris airport. At the bar while waiting to change planes, they were speaking broken French to each other for about forty minutes, when they realised they were both Scots and both blushed with embarrassment.

I often have a giggle picturing that scene.

'Well Joe, I am getting hungry now, let's go and eat.'

We sat down in the restaurant and I ordered the steak.

'The waitress asked in French, 'How would like your steak done?'

'Bien cuit s'il vous plaît.' (Well done.)

The meal came on an oval plate. No, I stand corrected, the steak came on the plate, the rest came separately.

There was, how I can say? Yes, a bucket of chips (French fries), a large bowl of peas, sweet corn, carrots and a basket of bread.

I turned to Joe and said, 'We will never eat all this.'

He laughed and said, 'No, we will not, because that's yours.'

'This waitress must be madly in love with me, or, she thinks I am starving,' I told him.

Joe said, 'I think it's love, you do not look as though you have been neglected. Bon appétit.'

I managed the steak, a few chips and a spoon-ful of peas and that was that.

When we had finished Joe said, 'One more drink and then its home to bed. I have work to go to in the morning.'

We had our last drink, I thanked him for a great night, but I could not manage anymore.

'I am going to bed now. Bon nuit.'

All I can say is, it's a good thing the motel was not that far away. I do not even remember walking back or getting into bed. I must have been well oiled, or as they say over here, "feeling no pain".

Waking up next morning I thought it was quite early. Early! Looking at the clock, it's 9.45 a.m. I have missed half the morning.

I got straight out of bed, showered and dressed and left the room. I looked up and down the street for somewhere to have my breakfast. There was a coffee pot diner across the road, so that's where I made for.

I think I will have some sweet coffee and pancakes with maple syrup. I am enjoying a different breakfast from the usual eggs, bacon, beans and so on.

After finishing my meal I thought that will put me right for a couple of hours, and went straight over to the garage.

'Morning, Joe. How are you this fine morning?'

'Très bien, merci. You have slept in a little, yes?'

'Yes,' I said a bit sheepishly. 'We had a good night, didn't we?' I said laughing.

'We certainly did, mon ami. What did you do after you left,' he asked?

'Wouldn't you like to know?' I smiled. 'Come on, let's get started, Joe. I want to learn as much as I can today, or what is left of it.'

'Have you had something to eat?' he enquired.

'Yes, thank you, I am ready for the day now.'

'Good, then I have some work for you. Come on round the back, I have got everything ready, including the horses. Right,' he said, 'what do you know about horses?'

'To be honest, bugger all,' I replied.

'Well,' he said. 'First, if you have not done much horse riding I would advise you to take some talcum powder with you.'

'What will I do with that?' I enquired.

'You will find out soon enough. We had better get started then. First I will show you how to saddle up.'

He showed me how to saddle up and put things in the right order, and also how to calm them down if necessary and the general ins and outs of dealing with horses.

The funniest thing that happened was when I went round to the back of the horse, it let off an enormous fart.

'Christ, that was a beauty.' We both started to laugh.

'It reminds me of the old sixty-nine joke,' I said.

'I have never heard that one,' said Joe.

'Oh, it's about a farmer, someone like you.

He had a twenty-four year old son who had never been with a woman.

'The farmer gave the son three hundred dollars and told him to go into the big city and get a woman of the night.

"What do you mean?" asked the son.

'The farmer told him to go to this certain district in the city and he would find out for himself.

"Stay the weekend," his father said.

'This the lad did, and on the first night, sure enough, he was picked up by one of the girls.

"Would you like a good time?" she asked.

"I don't know what you mean," he said.

"Come to my place and I will show you. It will cost you forty dollars."

"Okay," said the lad, and off they went.

'Back at the apartment he said, "What do you want me to do now?"

"Have you never done this before?" she asked.

"No," he said. "I have never ever been with a woman."

"Leave it to me," she replied. "We will start with a sixty-niner."

"What is that?" he enquired.

"Get undressed and lay on the bed."

'This the lad did and she started with a sixty-niner. She had just started when she let off a small fart.

"I am so very sorry," she said. She then went to the washroom, had a shower, came back and she started again when the same thing happened.

"To hell with this," said the farmer's boy. "I can't stand another sixty-seven of those."'

I thought Joe was going to wet his pants.

'Have you never heard that one before?'

'No, never,' he replied, with tears running down his cheeks.

I worked hard all day repeating some operations over and over so as to get them right.

I did not want to struggle on the journey or out at the cabin.

'You have done really good today,' said Joe. 'You must be tired now.'

'Yes, I am. I could use a rest before I go out tonight, if you know what I mean,' I said with a wink.

'Okay, there is not much more I can teach you today. We have done all we can in the time we had, so it's up to you now.'

'How much do I owe you for all your help, Joe?'

'You joke with me?' he replied.

'No, why do you say that?' I asked.

He smiled. 'You can settle up when you get back. I have only known you for about thirty hours and I think you are crazier than me. I have enjoyed your company,' he added, 'and would like to think we are friends now. Besides you paid for the meal last night. You owe me nothing.'

Well, was that a back handed compliment or what?

I don't mind telling you, this came as a pleasant surprise and I felt quite touched, especially being out here on my own. But that's the way over here. If they like you they treat you as one of the family.

'I will have everything ready tomorrow for you,' Joe said. 'I have marked the trail on the map and where to stay tomorrow night. The horses are ready when you are.'

I shook that big hand again (with a bit of caution this time).

'I will see you in the morning. I don't know what time, I will see how tonight goes first,' I said with a big smile.

I heard his gruff laugh as I walked away and started to do the same. We just seemed to hit it off.

Back at the motel I had a shower and lay on the bed with all sorts of things going thought my head. Saddling the horses, the trip, Joe, Mike and, of course, dinner tonight with Nadine.

I was looking forward to relaxing with a beautiful woman, a nice meal and just one bottle of wine. I really need to keep a reasonable clear head for my journey tomorrow.

Next thing I know the phone is ringing. The fresh air, work and the warmth of the room had knocked me right out.

I had to look around for the phone; I was still half asleep.
'Hello,' I said.

'Bonsoir, it's Nadine. What time would you like to dine?'

'Hello, Nadine, thank you for calling. Would eight o'clock be okay with you?'

Nadine said, 'You sound tired.'

'I was resting from my hard day's work.'

'Hard day's work? What have you been doing?'

'Joe's had me saddling and anything else to do with a horse for most of the day.'

'You call that hard work?'

'Okay. It is when you have never done it before.'

'In answer to your question. Eight o'clock will do fine,' she said.

'Good,' I replied. 'Do I need to book a table?

'No,' she said, 'I have made arrangements and will see you there.'

'Right that's a date. I am looking forward to seeing you there.'

I lay for a little while longer thinking life's not too bad is it. After all, when you look at the full picture, we are entitled to nothing, especially with all the nastiness going on in the world.

Yes, I'm feeling rather good. Right, get off your lazy arse, get showered, shaved and put on some decent clothes.

With my fresh clean clothes and aftershave on I was ready for the night.

I walked into the Arc-en-Ciel at 7.45 p.m. I did not want to be late for this date.

Having looked around, Nadine was nowhere to be seen. I thought it was too good to be true, I did not think she would turn up. So it looks like a glass of wine at the bar for a start, something to eat, and an early night.

Before going into the bar, I went to the doorway of the restaurant to have a look around to make sure Nadine was not there.

It was quite a classy place. One of those places where they ask how many and then find you a table. A young man behind a desk asked me if I would be dining tonight.

'Yes, I hope so, but not just now.' I answered. 'I am waiting for someone.'

'May I ask who, sir?' he said.

'Nadine, from the motel,' I replied.

'Oh yes, sir, I know her quite well. She has booked a table.'

'Would you tell her I am in the bar if and when she arrives, please?'

'Yes sir.' He smiled.

In the bar I had just been served with my drink, when Nadine walked in.

'Make that two, please,' she said.

This was a pleasant surprise, as I had not really expected her to turn up.

She looked even better when dressed up. Boy did she look good.

'Bonsoir, Nadine, you look nice.'

'Merci beaucoup, monsieur.'

'Comment allez-vous sur soir?'

'Can we speak English please?' I said. 'At least for the first part of the night.'

She looked puzzled.

'Oh, it's a long story, do not ask.' I said.

'Of course, I would like that very much.'

That's twice she has said that to me.

I do not think I can go far wrong here. I think she likes me, which makes a nice change for me. Nearly everything I do goes wrong. I had a rocking horse when I was a kid, and it died. That's how lucky I am.

'Okay,' I said, 'let's go into the restaurant where we can settle down.

'A waiter picked up our drinks and followed us to our table, then handed us a menu each.

'Bon appétit,' he said.

'Would you like a starter, Nadine?'

'Oui. I mean, yes please.'

The same waitress from the night before came over to take our order.

With a big smile on her face she said, 'Bonsoir, you are feeling good? Yes? Do you want to order now, please?'

'Good evening,' I replied, trying to be a little sophisticated.

Well you do when you're on a first date with someone you fancy. Also, I cannot remember all that I did last night.

Nadine ordered a salad and I had the soup of the day. I never thought of asking what soup it was. When it was served I enquired what it was.

'Cabbage soup, sir,' was the reply.

I had never heard of cabbage soup and I didn't fancy it at all, but it's served now and I will eat it. I took a spoonful and what a pleasant surprise, it was beautiful.

To follow, Nadine ordered ècrevisse which are freshwater crayfish.

'You should try these, they are very good,' she said.

'I would love to but I am allergic to fish.'

'Oh, that's too bad,' she answered.

I did not want the steak again so I ordered, 'Poulet, avec pommes de terre, et une bouteille de Chardonnay, s'il vous plaît.'

Nadine smiled and said, 'I thought we were speaking English tonight?'

'Oh, I beg your pardon. It's with everyone else speaking French, I just seemed to slip into it.

She remarked, 'I think you speak better French than we do.'

I asked how long had she worked at the motel.

'I have owned it for five years now.'

'You own it?'

'Yes, does that surprise you?' she asked.

'No, not really, I can imagine you as the boss.'

'How do I take that? She smiled.

'As a compliment,' I said.

The wine came and I poured us each a glass.

'How you say in England? Cheers,' said Nadine.

'Yes, same to you.'

It was nice to take time over the meal and get to know each other better.

I loved listening to her broken English. Sometimes it made me want to laugh, but I thought better of it. I was so relaxed, the evening was going so well. Her soft voice, the smell of her perfume and her feminine ways went down very well with me. As I said, taking time over the meal and the conversation made the night for me. We did not hurry and we lost track of time.

'We should go now,' she said. 'We are the last in the restaurant and they are waiting to close.'

I really had not noticed, the time had gone so fast and I was enjoying every minute.

'Do you stay at the motel?' I asked.

'No, I have my own house just on the edge of town.'

'How will you get home?' I enquired.

'I will go home by taxi.'

'Do you have one ordered, Nadine?'

'There is no need, there should be one outside.'

'Let me walk you to the taxi then?' I asked.

'Will you not join me for a coffee at my house?' she asked.

'I would like that very much, it would finish the night off nicely.' And for me at least, I thought to myself.

Sure enough there was a taxi outside.

It took about five or six minutes to get to her place. As we entered the drive I noticed a name plate. It had on it in big red letters COTERO. The driveway was about 200 yards long and had very tall pine trees on either side. As we approached the house it looked like a chalet from the outside.

She paid the taxi driver and we went in.

Once inside, the house was much bigger than it looked from the outside, very much bigger. All the floors were wooden, and it had a wood fire burning in a huge grate (just).

'Excuse me while I get some more logs for the fire,' Nadine said.

'By all means,' I replied I love a log fire. Let me help you.'

'No thank you. You get comfortable. Take off your coat and relax, I will get the logs and make some coffee.'

'Thank you. I will do just that if you don't mind.'

I picked up the local paper and had a scan through it

while Nadine put the logs on the fire, then she left the room to make coffee.

By the time she came back the fire was burning great. She was now dressed casually.

'The fire is going well,' she said.

'Yes, it certainly is,' I replied. 'It really makes the house comfortable.'

She went to put the coffee tray down on the table.

'Here, let me give you a hand,' I said.

As I bent forward to help her our cheeks were about one inch from one another. I could not stop myself from kissing her on her left cheek.

'Is that the best you can do?' she asked.

'No, not really, put the tray down and I will show you.'

Much to my surprise she did, and stood there waiting.

I took her in my arms and kissed her fully on the lips. The kiss seemed to last for about five minutes, and it felt so good.

'Are you bothered about your coffee?' Nadine asked.

'Not now I'm not.'

She took me by the hand and led me to the bedroom. I felt just like a teenage boy. I was all excited and it took all my restraint from grabbing her there and then but I did not want to spoil the night.

I could smell her perfume and the lights in the bedroom were down low.

We started to kiss again. I did not want to stop but Nadine said, 'Please will you undress me slowly.'

I do not know how I managed to go as slow as I did, but I was so glad I did. She was really beautiful undressed; she did have a wonderful figure.

It must have taken all of ten seconds to undress myself and get into bed with her.

I was very aroused and turned to Nadine and started to kiss and fondle her breasts. We then made love for what seemed like most of the night, after which we fell asleep in each other's arms.

I awoke next morning to the smell of fresh coffee and I could hear Nadine softly humming to herself.

'Bonjour, Nadine,' I called from the bedroom.

'Bonjour. Would you like some eggs and bacon for your breakfast?' she asked. 'Coffee is on the stove.'

'Could I have pancakes please, with maple syrup?'

'Yes, no problem.'

'That would be great. May I take a shower?'

'Why most certainly. There are plenty of towels, please help yourself. The shower room is on the right.'

I had my shower, got dressed and went into the kitchen. There Nadine was making my pancakes. I put my arms around her and kissed her on that left cheek again.

She turned to face me and kissed me fully on my lips. 'Thank you for a lovely time,' she said. 'Now let me finish cooking your meal.'

I very nearly said forget the breakfast, let's go back to bed.

Before I could say anything, Nadine said, 'You are leaving this morning are you not?'

'Well, I was going to set off today, but I might change my mind.'

'Don't stay because of me please, I will see you when you come back this way. I hope!'

'You most certainly will,' I said. 'I would like to stay with you for a while. That's if you would like me to of course.'

She kissed me again, and said, 'I want you to stay when you get back, now go and sit down, your breakfast is nearly ready.'

We looked into each other's eyes and a broad smile lit up my face.

'No,' she said, 'sit down.'

'I did not say anything.'

'You did not have to, just the look on your face said it all.'

While I was having my breakfast Nadine got ready to go to the motel. The breakfast was excellent and the coffee just as good. I cleared the table and was waiting for Nadine to appear.

She came out of the bedroom looking splendid as usual. I could feel myself getting excited all over again. I just had to kiss her.

'Where did you learn to kiss like that?' she asked. 'It makes me go weak at the knees.'

'Do you have to go to work?' I whispered.

'I'm afraid I do,' she said. 'But you must promise me you will stay with me when you get back.'

'You try and stop me,' I said.

'Come, I will drive you into town. Where do you want me to drop you off?'

'You had better make it the motel and I will change and pack, ready for the off.'

I asked her once again should we not stay here for the day.

'I have a business to take care of,' she said, 'and you have made arrangements.'

'Okay,' I reluctantly agreed and let go of her, and that was not easy the way I was feeling.

We drove into town and she stopped at the motel. Before getting out of the car we kissed goodbye.

'I will see you in about two weeks. I am going to miss you.'

Nadine said, 'Au revoir, not goodbye. Please look after yourself for me.'

After packing I walked over to Joe's garage.

'Morning Joe, how are things with you?'

'Bonjour. You look like the cat that got the cream. You must tell me all about it.

'I'm afraid not Joe. You will have to use your imagination, but I did have a wonderful evening.'

'Okay,' he said. 'Everything is ready and it looks like you have got a very good day to start with. When are you leaving?

'Now,' I said.

'Good, I will load the packhorse while you saddle the other, then you can get on your way.'

It took about one hour to get everything packed and ready.

I turned to Joe and said, 'Well, this is it, all systems go. All I have to do now is get mounted and be off. Thank you very much Joe you have been marvellous.'

'You are very welcome, my friend,' came the reply. 'We have had two good days together.'

We shook hands and a few minutes later I was on my way.

'You be careful,' he shouted after me, 'and we will have a drink when you get back.'

'That's a deal. See you then.'

He turned and went back into the garage.

I was still thinking of Nadine and the night we had just spent, when I realised how bloody wide this horse was. Was this a fat horse? Or are they all like this? Christ, I thought, I hope I can get used to this real soon otherwise it's going to hurt me more than the fat horse.

I took the map out of the saddle bag and looked at it for a while. It seemed quite straight forward. While I had been looking at the map I had crossed two large fields and found myself in the woods. They seemed quite thick, although the trail was very clear.

Joe was right about the horses, they just kept going down the trail without any instructions from me. I would keep going until about an hour before nightfall. That would give me some daylight to set up camp. That's if I am not split in half by then. About one and half hours later I had to get off this fat thing and walk a little, just to give my legs and my arse a rest.

The trail led me to a medium sized lake. It was as smooth as a mirror and I could see the reflections of the trees right around it. The colours were staggering, red, orange, yellow and brown.

I sat beside the lake for about fifteen minutes in wonder. Although I had only left civilisation a couple of hours ago, it felt like I was the only person in the world. The only things that moved were the birds and a slight breeze in the top of the trees. I would like to bring Nadine out here one day if only for a picnic. Then I thought what a lovely place to build a log cabin. Maybe one day I will do just that. Enough of dreaming, it's time to get going.

I climbed back onto Fatso very gingerly, this I was not

looking forward to. But I will have to get used to it if I am to get anywhere.

I noticed the temperature was dropping fast, so I put on my parka which I had bought especially for the trip. Boy did that make one hell of a difference. I had the horses trotting for a while and that warmed us all up nicely, besides making headway.

It's time for me to take another walk now and decide where to stop for the night. Looking at the place Joe had marked on the map for me to stay tonight I don't think I can be far off now, so if necessary it's back on to the fat one and do some more trotting.

I had no sooner thought it when I came to a clearing. This has got to be the place. He had described it so well, the big uprooted tree on the right hand side, a place where people had made camp fires before and a pile of old logs.

"Try to replace any logs you might use." I remember him saying.

'Okay, Fatso and friend, let's get this gear off you two, then you can do your own thing until the morning.'

I must get a fire going, I need a hot drink and something to eat and warm up a bit before I bed down for the night.

It did not take long to get the fire on the go. While it was burning nicely I walked down to the lakeside for some water to make the coffee.

Whilst drinking my coffee, which tasted like nectar, I suddenly realised how tired and sore I felt. It must have been the ride and fresh air. I was ready for bedding down now.

Before I do I should put some more logs on the fire and

use some of that talc on the inside of my thighs which were red raw. That's why Joe suggested the talc, he said I would find out the hard way.

I climbed into my sleeping bag and do not remember putting my head down, that's how fast I fell asleep.

Waking up next morning it was already bright and sunny and I thought, well that's what I call a good night's sleep.

When I tried to move I was as stiff as a board.

Oh no, I thought. It's a long time since I have felt like this. Come on, I said to myself, get up, have a cold wash in the lake, get some water at the same time for a brew, then have some breakfast.

The water was bloody cold and soon woke me up. I think the best thing to do is to walk for the first hour just to loosen up.

As soon as I started to move, the horses walked from the other side of the clearing, they seemed to know it was time to go.

'Good morning, Fatso and friend,' I said to them. Then thought, yes, they will answer, they can do everything else.

I have been on the trail one day and I find myself talking to the horses. What will I be like after two weeks? As long as they do not answer back I will be okay.

After having something to eat and drink I realised that I did not really feel the cold when I was sleeping. That's a good sign I thought.

I saddled up my trusty steed. That's a laugh, it's more like the one our coalman used. One that would just plod along all day like Fatso here.

The two packs that went on the other horse were well designed; you just throw them over the horse's back and tied the leather straps together, so that did not take long.

'Hi ho Silver.' I started to walk and they followed me with their heads down and without a worry in the world.

About fifty minutes down the trail, I don't know why, but Fatso was trying to tell me something. Both horses had their heads held high and their ears pricked. I had no idea why, but I felt things were not quite safe hereabouts; they both seemed very agitated.

'Okay Fatso,' I said as I mounted, 'let's do some trotting and get away from here.'

As soon as we started to trot they seemed to relax. They had obviously heard, smelt or felt something that I had not.

The country we were travelling through seemed so vast and as I said earlier I could not get over the colours. This is paradise, it feels really good to be here.

It's time for me to walk again. My legs and my arse tells me so and I agree.

'Come on, Silver and Scout, follow me.' (As if they needed telling.)

You would think I have all the time in the world the way I was dawdling, but I hope to be at the cabin sometime late tomorrow afternoon. I plan to have two or three day's rest when I get there, then I will go off for a day, maybe two and look around the area. Perhaps camp a couple of nights further out, come back and finish the holiday at the cabin, then make my way back to Nadine.

The day went very fast and the sun is starting to go down now. That night I camped by a stream and again the only thing I could hear was the breeze, the stream and the wild life. It felt like I was dreaming.

I had wanted to do this sort of thing for a long time and

now I am actually living out this dream.

If I could make a wish come true for everyone, it would be that they could achieve their one wish before they get too old. This, money cannot buy; the feeling is incredible.

It was the same routine as last night only things went a bit smoother. Tonight I would sleep in my small tent as it felt a lot colder than last night and I could see the frost falling. The horses wandered along the bank of the stream, where I got my water from. I lit a fire and got the coffee pot on.

Whilst the coffee was brewing I laid out my sleeping bag ready, knowing I would be out like a light as soon as I climbed into it.

I thought that after that experience earlier today, when the horses got frightened, I will get the rifle out and leave it next to me while I slept.

For the last two days I had not even looked at my watch. I had no idea of the time until I looked; it was only 5.45 p.m. I thought it might have been around 9.00 – 9.30 p.m. I can't remember the last time I went to bed this early, but it was to bed I was going straight after my coffee and snack.

Again I slept well. I'm still stiff so I will do the same as yesterday, walk for the first thirty minutes or so. After breakfast, which was sausages, a full tin of beans, some bread and coffee I was ready for anything.

'Come on you two, let's get going.' There I go again, talking to those two. I would not mind so much but the only reply I seemed to get off Fatso is the occasional fart. I think he's eating beans as well.

It's another sunny morning, the sky is blue and clear; everything feels so fresh. Today I should reach the cabin, all being well. I've decided to keep going until I get there. No more dawdling, let's get the show on the road, or should I say trail?

I am managing to stay in the saddle a little longer now, still sore but not as bad, now that I am getting used to it.

It was about 2.30 p.m. when I came out of a very thick part of the forest.

There in front of me was the cabin. It was built in a clearing on the edge of a stream.

'Come on you two, we are there, let's get unpacked and relax for a couple of days.'

We trotted down to the cabin, I rode around it to have a look and I was impressed.

Mike had done a good job of building it. There was a small corral at the back for the horses. A lean-to with plenty of firewood and from the outside it looked very clean.

Sure enough once inside it was like a little palace. Mike obviously cleans and puts everything away before leaving. I made a mental note to do the same; it's the least I can do.

Meanwhile the first thing is to get a fire going to get the place warmed up. It had an ample fire place; I can have a decent size fire in this I thought.

I waited until the fire was going well then went back out to unsaddle the horses. I gave them a brush down, fed them and let them wander at their leisure for at least the next two days.

I checked the fire again. It was burning nicely so I would have a walk outside to have a good look around.

Boy, was it quiet, just Mother Nature, me, Fatso, farting, and friend. Fatso reminds me of my mate, Mike, he is always farting.

There was a small hill behind the cabin. I thought I would have a walk up there and have a look around to see what I can see. It only took about fifteen to twenty minutes to get to the top.

Other than this hill I was stood on, the area seemed to be quite flat. There was a larger hill or mountain, about ten to twelve miles away to the right of the cabin as I look down from this hill.

The sun is setting to the left of it, the rest was all forest and very thick it looked too, other than around the cabin which Mike had obviously cleared to make the cabin.

There was a very big lake on the other side of the hill on which I was stood. Maybe when I have rested up I will have a ride around it for something to do.

I must have been up there for an hour or so. It was the hunger that reminded me I had not stopped for lunch, so back to a warm cabin to make myself a meal. I might even try a drink out of that bottle Mike gave me.

I unpacked the saddle bags and put things away ready for use. There was ample cupboard space and furniture.

I had forgotten to air the bedding so it's the sleeping bag again tonight. First thing in the morning, I will hang all the bedding over the fence outside, that's if the weather permits.

I had my meal, tidied up, built up the fire and thought, I will have one more walk around before I settle down for the night. Outside it was very cold and the horses were in a stall at one end of the corral, which I imagined would keep them quite warm. There were all sorts of noises going on, which I did not recognise. I guess it's the wildlife doing their thing.

I said, 'Goodnight, Fatso and friend, see you in the morning.' (Boy, am I getting there or what?)

The night was very still and the moon was shining very brightly and it seemed that every star in the universe was out, each one brighter than the other. I would like to think that was a welcome sign for me.

Right, enough of this I am off to the cabin and hopefully a good night's rest. Walking into the cabin the warmth felt comforting. I will now have to sort out my sleeping bag.

I put the bag on the bed ready for use, opened the bottle Mike had given me and poured myself a drink. Not thinking I took a gulp of the contents. When I got my breath back I shouted, 'Holy shit!' This cannot be for human consumption, it must be for putting on cuts the horses get. Just wait until I see that big ape Mike.

He should have put a warning notice on it. Something like a skull and crossbones would be suitable. I made a pot of coffee and drank that to take the vile taste away.

God, I'm feeling tired now, just let me get into that bag (yes, the sleeping bag), I have no energy for anything else.

It did not take long for me to get to sleep as usual.

I was awakened two or three times during the night by some strange noises. I have no idea what they were and I was too tired to care, and sleeping in a strange bed did not help.

Next morning I was out of bed at 6.45 a.m. and making my breakfast when I heard something outside the door. I opened it very slowly and there was a racoon. I opened the door fully and the racoon just looked up at me and walked away without a care in the world, my size did not seem to bother him. Well, I thought, that's my first contact with one of the locals and if they are all as friendly as him it's going to be a nice stay.

The smell of bacon reminded me of what I was doing, so it's back to the stove and let's get down to the business of feeding myself. The sun was up and it's a fine morning so I sat on the front step with my plate on my lap.

I had just finished eating when Fatso and friend walked up to the cabin.

'Morning men, and what have you two been up too? (Christ there I go again.) I will not need you two today, but if you like we can have a walk together and you can show me around the place. How does that sound?'

The reply was one of Fatso's farts.

'Okay, if that's the way you feel I said I will walk around by myself.

I washed the few pots I had used and then put on my winter clothing. When I came back out the horses were still there. I walked past them and they turned and followed me without hesitation.

'Come on then, let's walk along the river for a while and see what we can see. You know the place better than me.'

I kept on walking for quite a while and found that the river meandered around the hill I had stood on last night. The air was so fresh and there was very little wind and it felt really good to be alive.

I must have walked for a good hour or so drinking in the scenery, not listening to anything in particular, then all of a sudden I heard the two horses galloping away.

I turned around to see them heading back toward the cabin with their heads and ears up.

'What's up with you two?' I shouted after them. 'Is there something around you do not like?'

I had no sooner said it but as I turned to carry on, it was

then I saw what had frightened them. It was a big black bear about 150 yards away on a bend in the river. It seemed to be fishing and did not see me, plus as I said, there was very little wind so it can't have got my scent. It was then that I noticed that what little wind there was, was coming toward me. And that's how the horses had picked up his scent!

I walked slowly over to a tree and stood behind it for a while watching.

The bear was in and out of the water like a water baby, no bother at all and it was catching some big fish. Then I noticed the bear taking the fish to the river bank, where there were two little fellows he or she was feeding. I believe it must have been a she as they are usually the ones who look after the young.

I watched absolutely fascinated for some time, the little fellows looked just like the teddy bears you can buy in the toy shop.

I reckoned I was about three miles from the cabin. I walked backwards for a few yards keeping the tree between me and the bears. Then made my way back to the cabin,

When I arrived the two deserters were in the stall; thanks a lot for waiting for me, I could have done with a lift back. Later that day I realised I will have to start carrying the rifle if I go walking or riding again, just in case. After all I don't know what I might meet and I should be prepared.

After a nice meal I put the bedding onto the bed ready for tonight, unpacked my supplies and put the food in the cupboards. There was a lot of tinned food and cans of beer already there, so I was not going to go hungry. Also, I could have a decent drink instead of that horse liniment, which I think I will do tonight. I had worked for about two hours but it was worthwhile and now I think I deserve that beer I promised myself.

As I sat drinking my beer I thought, this is more like it, I can relax for the rest of the day and tomorrow.

I noticed the sun going down so I built up the fire and went for a last look around before I settled down for the night. I walked to the top of the hill which has become my favourite place already. It was so quiet and the only thing that reminded me of civilisation was a vapour trail a jet had left while speeding through the sky.

The smoke from the cabin chimney seemed to be telling me, come back, get warm and have your beers.

Yes, that's a good idea. I had not realised how cold I was as I sat there dreaming.

Walking back I noticed how the ice was crackling under foot, it was really getting cold now winter is really setting in. I walked around the cabin checking that everything was in order and that the horses were okay. Do I say goodnight to them or not? Oh what the hell, I will make a deal with you two. I'll talk to you while I am on this adventure but keep it to yourselves.

'Goodnight boys, see you in the morning.'

Fatso farted as I walked away, I suppose that's better than nothing. The fire was burning brightly and the cabin had warmed up very nicely thank you, and tonight I will sleep in the all together like I normally do.

I woke up bright and early next morning and said to myself, well that was not a bad night's sleep, but I did feel the cold now and again so tonight I will sleep with my sweats on just to make me feel a bit more comfortable.

I have noticed I am enjoying my meals up here, especially

my breakfast and that's the main reason for getting out of bed. I suppose it's the fresh air and that bit of exercise riding up here, and the walk yesterday But first things first, let's get the fire built up then I can make the breakfast.

Today I will have a little ride for a couple of hours in the opposite direction to yesterday, and see what the countryside is like there. The fire was still burning slightly so it did not take long to get going. I made my breakfast and opened the door so as to eat on the front step, and there was the racoon again. He did not run away or anything, so I shared my bread with him or her.

I think from now on when I see an animal no matter what I will refer to it as it.

It turned out that the racoon shared the bread with me, as it got the most.

I then went back and sat at the table with the door open. It sat outside on the porch just like a pet dog would do. The horses came from the side of the cabin together; they seemed to disturb the racoon and it wondered off along the river bank into the woods. No doubt it will be back tomorrow looking for some more food,

After my breakfast I saddled up Fatso and put the rifle in the holder next to the saddle bags, hoping I will never have to use it, and set off into the woods.

We just dawdled along for a while. I was trying to take everything in. It was so lovely and so quiet and all that I could hear was Fatso's clip clop on the ground and his occasional fart. This horse should see a vet.

Just as we came to the edge of a clearing I could see some deer on the far side grazing, so I backed Fatso up a little and got off to watch with my binoculars.

They were beautiful animals with lovely delicate coats and big brown eyes. They seemed to be very wary, I think they must have heard or seen us. I had left Fatso about ten yards back in the woods, so they could not have seen him and I was well hidden behind a thick tree.

Now, their heads were up, their ears were pricked just like Fatso and friend did on the way here, and their eyes had widened. They were moving from one side of the clearing to the other in unison. When all of a sudden there was a crashing of trees from the far side of the clearing and out came a very big black bear.

The deer started to panic and run around blindly.

I thought the bear has no chance of catching one of them, but I have never seen anything so big, move so fast; it was incredible. The bear was moving fast, very fast indeed. Much to my surprise it did manage to catch one.

My first reaction was to run back to Fatso. Which I did. I took out the rifle, checked that it was loaded and ran back to shoot the bear. I had the bear right in my sights when I realised what I was doing. So I lowered the gun slowly.

I could only watch while Nature took her course and my heart sank a little watching this savage spectacle. It was not long before the deer stopped moving and I could watch no more as the bear tore it to pieces.

Again I backed up to where Fatso was, untied him and walked back quietly along the trail for some hundred yards or so, still thinking of what I had witnessed. It was then I realised, they must have scented me and Fatso on one side of the clearing and the bear on the other. That explains why they were moving like they had been.

Then I mounted Fatso for the ride back to the cabin. All the way back I kept thinking could I or should I have saved the deer.

I could not get the sight of it out of my mind, but after a while I knew the answer was no and I had done the right thing. However, I could not help thinking I had blocked off their escape route. It was not for me to interfere with nature, after all the bear was only looking after itself when all is said and done.

I found it all a bit scary, spectacular, and fascinating, all at the same time. I did not know what to make of it all.

Well, I have met a few of the locals now, the racoon, the deer and of course the bears.

The first two I would not mind meeting close up, but that's as near to a bear as I want to get.

It played on my mind for the rest of the day and most of the night and it put me off my meal.

So I just had a few beers and tried to think in terms of it being a privilege to witness such a sight; after all not too many people do.

Next morning I was a bit hung over and still a little tired, so it was my usual big breakfast and a pot of coffee. I will hang around the cabin today and make plans for my little trip and put out what

I will be taking.

The events of yesterday kept coming back from time to time, like a song you start to hum and cannot stop humming over and over again, but I was coming to terms with it now.

Life has got to go on. It did not exactly upset me but it does make you think deeper about life.

I have not done much today, I just got things ready for my trip. What I would take to eat and clothing, etc. I would include my sweats for sleeping in, take my little tent and so on. I drank lots of coffee. I lay down two or three times and had a lazy day; I enjoyed it. I have decided to go on Fatso and leave the packhorse behind, have two days or three at the most and then make my way back to the cabin.

Well, that was a lazy day. I have everything ready for tomorrow so I will have a couple of beers, and I mean two beers, and go to bed for an early night.

I built up the fire, had my two beers, drank them nice and slowly and got into bed. As usual I was asleep in no time.

Waking up next morning I felt very refreshed and raring to get on the way. I was looking forward to the ride, having given my thighs and legs a rest by not having ridden for two days, and to looking around the beautiful area.

After getting up that morning bright and early I had my breakfast, made sure the fire was out, got Fatso ready and my pack sorted.

Now all there is left to do is say so long to the packhorse and the racoon which had turned up again that morning.

'See you in two or three days,' I said, then locked up the cabin and got on my way.

I followed the river down to the lake which took most of the morning. When I finally reached the lake, which was quite a large one, it looked really beautiful with the sun dancing across it.

I stopped for a snack, and also to give my thighs and arse a rest again. I am still not used to riding Fatso, but I'm enjoying it more and more with the creaking of the leather and the sound of his hooves on the hard ground.

Sitting there on the edge of the lake having my snack I thought I would go to the far end of the lake then turn left into the forest. Don't ask me why, I just thought I would have a look along the edge of the lake, then some of the rest of the terrain before making my way back to the cabin. I planned to sleep out no more than three nights, most probably just two.

When I had finished eating I set off walking along the lake side. Again the scenery was breathtaking. The lake was as smooth as a mirror, the trees were of several different colours of late autumn and the sky its usual lovely blue. Not a cloud in sight and it is very quiet. The sun was bright but not very hot.

It was the sort of day I would like to share with everyone, but then again that would take away the very magic I was enjoying.

So I will take it all in and perhaps I can share it in some other way; maybe I could write about it when I get home, although I have never done that sort of thing before. I will think it over but for now I will just enjoy all the things around me.

I had walked for more than an hour and half and Fatso had just followed me; I had forgotten about him while I walked. It was a good thing he did know the routine backwards like Joe had said otherwise I would have to go all the way back for him.

Where that hour and a half went to I do not know. The time might have gone fast but the memory will stay with me forever.

Come on, Fatso, give me a ride to the end of the lake and then we will settle down for the night. I will make a fire to start with, and then I can have a nice drink of tea. Put a tin of Heinz sausages and beans on to heat, after which I will not take much rocking.

It took another hour to get to the far end of the lake where I found a grassy bank on the edge of the lake so I pitched the tent there.

After unsaddling Fatso, I built a fire, had my sausages and beans with my cup of tea, and boy did I enjoy it, and the tea tasted good as well. I had been drinking coffee most of the time I had been in Canada and brought the tea for a change and because it was light to carry, the powdered milk was not as good as fresh.

But it will do for now, it is serving the purpose. The sun was very low now just at the top of the trees, its orange glow laid along the lake like a carpet.

With the lake being so smooth it looked like I could have almost walked on it. This is another image I will treasure for a very long time, I only wish I had remembered to pack the camera. The fire was also getting low now so I put on some big logs to build it up for the night.

When it was well alight the fire did the same as the sun had done, just before it went behind the trees. Only the carpet from the fire was bright red and at right angles to where the sun had laid its carpet.

The reflection of these two colours on the lake, as I said, I will never forget.

I have never been religious but I could imagine something like this experience and the scenery I am going through could help one to change.

What or whoever created this, certainly knew what they were doing. It is truly wondrous and I feel so privileged to be here.

All of a sudden I was brought back to reality by one of Fatso's specials.

He was stood behind me with his great arse pointing my way. Thanks a lot, Fatso, I only wish I could return the compliment. Maybe I can later when the beans have done their job.

I was very tired now and ready for my sleeping bag, so it's goodnight, Fatso. Goodnight fire and the lake, I hope to see you in the morning.

I was awakened by the sound of falling water. Is that a heavy rain fall I thought? I climbed out of the sleeping bag, opened the tent flap, and there was Fatso having a pee next to the tent.

'Oh, come on Fatso. Is it something I've said or done. You said goodnight last night with one of your specials and now you say good morning by nearly peeing on me. Why could you not have done it in the woods like anyone else?'

He gave a shudder and walked away.

I had slept very well and was ready for the new day.

Although the sun was up and it was very bright I think this is the coldest I have felt since I have been in Canada. So first things first, let's have a fire going for starters before I do anything else.

I had a wash in the lake which I had done yesterday and loved it. It certainly woke me up; it was definitely a lot colder.

When I got back to the fire, the water was boiling nicely, so it was a mug of hot tea and something to eat.

I was saddling Fatso when I felt the beans working. 'Fatso,' I said while putting on his bridle, 'I have something for you.'

I let off one almighty fart. His nostrils flared. Fatso did not seem to think much of the gesture and tried to back away.

'Oh no you don't,' I said, holding the reins tightly. 'How do you like a taste of your own medicine? Not much, eh?'

I started to laugh out loud and let go of the reins. He walked a few yards away shaking his head. That made me worse and I laughed even more because it reminded me of another joke.

Whilst working in St John, at the lunch break one Canadian asked another, 'Do you have a match, buddy?'

'Yes I sure do,' said the other. 'Your breath and a buffalo's fart.'

Well, that was a good start to the day. Let's hope we can carry on from here.

The day seemed to go too fast, I did not take any notice of the time, I was too busy looking around and talking to Fatso and enjoying it in general. I reckoned we had covered a few miles.

He was quiet all day, maybe he was still sulking from this morning. I hope not because he was a few up on me.

Anyway, as I said, the day was over before we knew it, the forest was getting very thick and the weather was closing in on us a bit. It's time to pitch the tent and settle down for the night. I will see what it is like in the morning and if it is any worse I will turn back.

I will tell you this, the fresh air sure knocks me out, I did not hear a thing all night. I do not know if that's a good thing or not with being out here on my own. But if there was anything untoward I am sure Fatso would let me know no doubt.

Waking up next morning the sun was out and the sky had cleared. I know I have mentioned the sun several times, but you have to see it to appreciate what I am going on about.

So I thought I would have one more day in the saddle, sleep out here tonight, then I will head off back to the cabin tomorrow. I do not think there is much more I can see that's any different to what I've already seen and enjoyed. I feel I might spoil the trip if I go any further.

That day was just like the one before and again I lit a nice big fire at the night time.

Well, seeing as this is my last night out here I will have a swig of the horse liniment Mike gave me. This I did and sat for a while in the forest, just me and Fatso.

I had a look around again; looking around becomes a habit before turning in. Everything was quiet, so it's off to the tent and into the sleeping bag.

When I awoke the next morning I knew immediately that something was different, things did not feel the same somehow. When I opened the tent flap some snow fell into the tent. I climbed out. It was about two feet deep or more.

Hell, where had that come from? That was a daft question.

Well, it looks and feels like Christmas. It looked wonderful, everything was white. The trees, the ground, the sky, this is something else.

I have never seen so much snow all at once, only on a Christmas card.

Where I live in the north west of England on the coast we

get about two inches of snow at the most, and that is gone in about half a day,

Right, the first thing to do was to clear a bit of ground and light a fire with some pieces of a dead tree that was sticking up nearby.

Fatso was there behind the tent, he did not seem too bothered. I made a big snowball and threw it at him. It hit him squarely on the rump. He turned his head and looking at me with those big brown eyes as much as to say, that was a bit childish, even for you. I made a bigger breakfast then usual and drank a full pot of tea hoping it would set me up for the day ahead. I was as full as a gun.

Whilst I was having my meal, I realised that there was no trail to follow and no signs to tell me which way I had come from or was going to. I now began to wish I had turned back yesterday, but it's too late now.

While I sat there eating, I remembered pitching the tent with the opening facing the way I had come from, so that was a good start. I thought Fatso will know his way back, so I am not going to worry much about that at this stage.

The first thing to do after breakfast is get packed up and get on the way. Get a full day's travelling in and not to panic.

My nerves were a little on edge but the one thing that was drummed into me when I was learning to scuba dive was not, under any circumstances, to panic. So I will apply the same principle to this predicament.

Okay, I have had my breakfast and saddled Fatso and we are now ready for the off.

We took it steady at first. As I said before we set out I will give Fatso his head and see which way he takes. Sure enough he headed in the direction the tent opening had been facing. I was somewhat relieved to think that I had made a mental note of the direction we came from.

Now I think the hard part will be getting back the same way, because as I said, there were no signs of the trail, and everything is white. The going seemed to be hard and Fatso was struggling, so while we travelled through this thick wood we would just have to take it easy.

I think it's going to take a long time to get back to the cabin and I felt butterflies in my stomach. I had a funny feeling that getting back to the cabin was not going to be easy. I must keep my head and let Fatso do his best to get us home. I thought it would be a good idea if we stopped every hour, for fifteen minutes at least and let Fatso have a little rest.

By the end of that first day I could tell Fatso was really tired, he was getting too old for this. Christ why didn't I turn back yesterday when it was clear?

I feel it's a bit early to stop but I have got to let Fatso rest for the night. Hopefully we can get a very early start in the morning, go slowly but make more miles in the day.

I had to scratch around a little harder than usual for firewood. Everything was taking twice as long to do now. Just walking in the snow took a lot of effort; it's like walking on a water bed.

Talk about being hungry. I could eat a scabby cow; my stomach thinks my throat is cut.

Fatso stayed closer to the camp that night more than any other. He didn't seem to settle at all.

I kept waking up from time to time, I can't tell you why. Maybe it was with him moving around and I could either hear or feel him.

I awoke with a sudden jolt. It was Fatso going mad to get away. What on earth is it? I thought he was going to uproot the tree I had tethered him to.

'Calm down, I will be with you as soon as I can.' I scrambled out of the tent and took hold of his reins and stroked him for a while; he was scared of something.

'Okay! Fatso, I will saddle you up as quickly as I can and we will get away from here. I will have my breakfast later if that makes you feel any better.'

I knew from my short experience that all was not safe around here. He knows there is something wrong. He knows better than me, so the faster we get away from here the better. I had one hell of a job getting Fatso saddled, he was really on edge.

Anyway we were finally packed up and on our way. The going was still hard, but as I said we will just have to take it easy, but keep going.

We had been going for most of the morning when we came upon a clearing in the forest. It would be about as big as a rugby ground.

'Well Fatso, what do you think? Should we try and make up a little time and have a trot across this clearing?'

We started to trot, but about a quarter of the way across, Fatso then started to gallop without any instruction from me.

'What the hell is up with you?'

I had no sooner said it when his head went down and I flew over the top of him at a great speed. I landed on my back in the snow looking up at the sky. I was not hurt just a little winded.

I don't know why but I started to laugh out loud, I could see the funny side of the situation.

I lay there for about two minutes laughing, when I heard Fatso whinnying. I sat up but Fatso was still lying down.

'Come on you daft bugger, you've had your fun, get up and let's get on our way.'

It was then I realised there was something very, very wrong.

'Come on Fatso, don't mess about,' I said, fearing the worst.

I went over to him and stoked his neck.

'Come on, I need you. What's the problem?'

He just lay there looking up at me with his big brown eyes. So I examined him and much to my distress I found he had broken a front leg. He must have stumbled down a hole or something.

'Christ, why did you have to set off galloping like that for, you idiot? Look at the state you are in now.'

I think I said those words out of fear, sympathy, and with a feeling of sheer helplessness.

'Oh Fatso, what am I going to do now? I can't get you up and I can't fix your leg. We are both in real trouble now, are we not?'

The sun was starting to go down now and my mind is going ten to the dozen.

Calm down I said to myself, try and think more clearly.

I was comforting Fatso the best I could, when I noticed the reason he had started to gallop.

There were five, maybe six, wolves on the edge of the clearing.

Bloody hell, that's all I need right now.

They were keeping their distance, just beyond the tree line but I could see them all right. Fatso tried to get up, he obviously knew they were there and didn't like it one little bit.

'Okay Fatso, I have seen them, try and lie quietly, you are hurt enough. Let me think will you?'

I had lain there for a few minutes when Mike's words came to me.

"If you see any wolves, just let a shot off and they usually run away."

That's it. I will fire a shot over their heads and see what they do.

I stood up, took out the rifle, cocked it and fired in their direction aiming just over their heads. The sound was deafening, with everything being so quiet out here. The shot seemed to do the trick, they disappeared out of sight. At the same time the shot didn't seem to bother Fatso, he just lay there. I guess he has heard a gun many times before.

When I got myself together again and everything was quiet once more I decided that I would try and make Fatso a bit more comfortable by taking off the saddle and the saddle bags. I cleared the snow from around him the best I could; that's the least I can do.

He give out a whimper now and then, he was obviously in great pain. In the back of my mind, I knew what I had to do, but I tried not to think about that at this moment.

It was not long before the wolves were back. They were looking pretty mean and hungry so there was only one thing for it. I will give them something to eat. I will shoot one of them. I had never killed anything before, but things are getting desperate, it looked like me or them.

I picked out the biggest of the pack, took aim and fired. The shot picked the wolf up and threw it about three yards through the air; like an invisible hand had just discarded it. Again the others ran off, and again it was not long before they were back. Again the others ran off, and again it was not long before they were back.

This time they had their meal. There was one hell of a fight for the carcass; they were all trying to get their share.

It was darker now and things seemed to be quiet for the time being. I snuggled up to Fatso's back with my back against his. I left the blanket over him to make him more comfortable and could feel the warmth coming off his great body.

What am I going to do now I asked myself? I kept drifting off to sleep. It must have been a combination of all the things that had happened that day.

Before I knew, it was morning. I was awoken by Fatso moving,

'Are you okay, Fatso? No, I know you're not.'

The first thing I looked for was the wolves. They were still there, but they were all lying down now. Still keeping a watchful eye on us, they must know we are in trouble. They can take their time now and see what becomes of us.

I knew what I had to do and I was not looking forward to it. I took a big swig out of the bottle Mike had given me. It did not help me any as my stomach was in my mouth.

I pulled myself up, knelt next to Fatso's head and stroked his neck again. His big brown eyes looked at me; he seemed to know what I was going to do.

I have never been an animal lover, but at the same time I could never be cruel to anything either; this is breaking my heart. I pulled the blanket over his face. I don't think I can do this, but what was the alternative? I can't leave him to suffer and if I did the wolves will just rip him to pieces while he was still alive. Come on, do the right thing for him, get on with it.

I was getting angry at myself now, or was it nervousness. I think it's the latter. I cocked the rifle and the sound made Fatso try to get up; yes he knew all right. I placed the barrel about two inches from the middle of his head and pulled the trigger. His great body shuddered and then he lay still. I didn't even hear the sound of the shot.

I don't even know if the wolves ran away or not.

Everything was quiet now and I was all alone with my head spinning and my stomach churning. What am I going to do now? Which way do I need to go?

Slow down, I said to myself, just think for a minute. That's it. I looked back from where we had come from. I could see Fatso's hoof prints coming out of the forest in a straight line to where he had fallen, so I will carry on in the opposite direction. I suppose that's not a bad start, he must have known where he was heading,

First things first, what do I need to help me survive? I must keep a clear head.

I looked through the saddle bags, took out what food there was, not a lot I thought.

I will leave the tent, the saddle and the saddle bags, they were far too heavy to cart around.

There were four bars of chocolate, a couple of tins of food and that bottle, etc. I filled my pockets with what I could and had another drink; I would eat later when I have put some distance between me and the wolves.

Before I set off I thought, if I split Fatso open it will make it easier for the wolves and perhaps it would give me more time. I reckon there will be enough meat on him to last them a full week.

I checked my clothing, fastened everything up, took out my knife and taking a deep breath I slit Fatso open. His massive intestines fell out onto the ground, I thought I was going to be sick.

I set off and tried not to think about it but this was not easy.

I don't know if that had been the right thing to do, but it seemed to make sense to me at the time.

Don't ask me why, even I don't know, but there is nothing I can change now.

The going was heavy, very heavy. It must have taken about one hour just to get to the far edge of the clearing.

As I approached the tree line going into the forest, I turned around to have one last look at Fatso. Sure enough the wolves were edging closer to where he lay. I felt the anger well up inside of me. I felt like shooting the bloody lot of them, but that would be a waste of ammo.

Goodbye, Fatso, I am very sorry it turned out this way, for you and for me. I didn't mean all those things I said about you, I hope you can forgive me. You knew I was only joking.

Once in the woods, I have decided to keep to the routine, walk for forty-five minutes and rest for fifteen, this was so I didn't sweat too much.

I have read that if you sweat a lot, it will freeze the clothing to your body and then hypothermia will set in.

I hope I am doing things right. I will have to be very careful and pace myself. At this moment I feel like running like hell, but not in this thick snow, I will get nowhere fast.

It feels like when I was a little child, having a bad dream running and getting nowhere as though I'm running in thick treacle with someone chasing me. I think most of us have had that dream or something similar.

I don't think there will be any trouble from the wolves I left behind; they have plenty to eat for now. That's not to say I will not meet anymore on my way back to the cabin. I will have to keep a sharp eye open.

I had walked about three hours when I came upon a rocky outcrop, so I thought I would take a well-earned rest. I found a nice little cranny where the rocks were all around me. This would make a good place to stop for the night as I was protected on three sides.

I put down the rifle and flopped to the ground.

I guess I was really exhausted from everything that had occurred that day. Not just physically exhausted, but also mentally. I was very tired but my mind is still going round and around thinking of Fatso, the wolves and the hard going of getting back to the cabin.

I have no problem resting my body, it's my mind I'm having trouble getting to slow down. I think I'm going to get a headache if I don't control it soon, but that is easier said than done at the moment.

With that thought I fell asleep. I dreamt about letting Fatso walk across the clearing and not trot. I also kept dreaming of the two carpets, the orange and red on the lake. Don't ask why, but they kept coming into my mind.

They seemed to be keeping me warm, very warm indeed in my dream. It must have been psychological.

I awoke with a start.

That's it! I thought I was bloody freezing. I had fallen asleep without lighting a fire. With everything on my mind and being so exhausted, I had obviously just laid there and nodded off.

Although it was early morning, about 2.30 a.m., with the moon and the snow it was still fairly light. I had to get moving to warm myself up. If I can find some firewood I will light a fire and have something to eat. I was so hungry, with everything that had gone on; I had not even had a meal that day. I hope not to repeat that again.

It was a bit of a struggle to find any wood that would burn; just looking for it warmed me up nicely. Once the fire had got going I made myself a meal and enjoyed every bit of it; the cranny trapped most of the heat off the fire.

It was quite comfortable, too comfortable in fact. I started to think of Fatso again and all that had happened that day, everything kept going round and around in my head, like a film or a piece of music over and over you can't stop.

I nodded off again, but this time I had a good three hours' sleep.

When I woke up the sun was on the rise, it looked good to me. It gave me a warm feeling. I decided to stoke up the fire and have a big mug of sweet tea to get me on my way.

This I did, it tasted good, and I was well rested and ready to make tracks.

Obviously my first task was getting back to the cabin. I stood for a while getting my bearings before setting off. I had made a note of which way I was going and I could see where I had come from. I only hope it was the right way.

If I am to stay out many more nights, I would not mind staying in a place like the one I had just stayed in, but that's a bit too much to ask.

Right, I said to myself. Forget about yesterday, but that's not going to be easy. I must concentrate on the job in hand, and focus on staying alive now and getting back. I feel completely alone, just a little sad and feeling a bit forlorn. Maybe even a little sorry for myself.

That's not going to do any good at all is it? Right let's get going.

Every time I stopped, I looked back to see if I was travelling in a straight line from where I had come. The time seemed to go so fast, two or three hours with the rest periods seemed nothing.

Was it that my mind is still busy? Or was it that I had chosen the right tactics? Walk for forty-five minutes, rest for fifteen. I have also decided to stop for one hour at around midday, just like a working day. I obviously cannot keep going all day that would be foolish.

I was also thankful that I was fairly fit with all the swimming and walking I had done. Still it was very hard going, even for me.

As I said the time went quickly, it was soon midday, my rest period is here. I would try and find a fallen tree sticking up from the snow to sit on. Although while I was walking the time went quickly, while I sat for my break the time seems to go a lot slower.

I had to check myself from setting off too early. A bit of

discipline will be needed to keep to the plan. The last thing I need is to rush when I know I should not.

Sitting there, I thought of the two carpets again. Why is this? Was it the lovely glow they gave out across the lake? Or was it that I wished I was still there with Fatso; wishing I had turned back then?

Although it is very cold, I had very good winter clothing. With that and the walking I kept reasonably warm.

Looking at my watch, my hour had gone, plus I was getting chilly sitting there. Time to walk some more to get warmed up again. Come on, give it another forty-five minutes I said to myself.

The sun was high now, bright pale yellow and not much heat coming off it. There's not much chance of it melting the snow I thought. It reminds me of John Denver singing, "Sunshine on My Shoulders". But this is no concert or picnic.

If I get out of this I will go to see John Denver in concert, with a bit, not a lot of luck. Well that's as good a reason to survive is it not?

The combination of the forty-five and fifteen was a good one, it mixed progress with resting. I really enjoyed the fifteen minutes rest, because it did not hold me up for too long. That day was uneventful and I just made what progress I could.

I was feeling the cold more and more now.

Was it because I did not have enough to concentrate on? That's a laugh.

Or was it that the weather was getting colder?

Whichever it was, I could do nothing about it.

That night I lay under the branches of a fir tree. The lowest leaves were only two feet off the ground and when I crawled under them, they were like a roof over my head.

With it being so cold I decided to try and wake up every two hours.

I could always do that sort of thing, I must have an internal clock or something like that; then again I suppose everybody does. When I was working and going out with the lads staying up till one and two o'clock in the morning, I would say to myself before going to sleep, don't forget it's work in the morning, don't sleep in. Sure enough, I would wake up about half an hour before the alarm clock went off.

Let's hope it works out here.

I did wake up every two hours, but I think it had more to do with the cold than my internal clock. I would want to set off again as soon as possible, getting on my way and getting warmed up at the same time. But I talked myself into sticking to the routine.

When I woke that morning the first thing I said was, 'Come on, Fatso, let's have you saddled, you lazy fat sod. We need to put some miles in.'

Then it dawned on me he was no longer there.

Was I starting to hallucinate? Or was it just a force of habit? I hope it is the latter.

When I had pulled myself together I got on the way, I didn't even have any breakfast.

This was becoming a bit of a ball ache, trudging through this bloody rubbish. It's getting harder and harder, but what else can I do?

Two and a half hours later I stopped for something to eat. I took out my last tin of sausages and beans. I decided to eat them cold I just cannot be bothered to look for any firewood. It's too much like hard work now. Bollocks to it.

Come on now don't start to lose it, try and keep a grip on yourself. Sit in the sun, relax for a few minutes and get your breath before starting off again. As a sat there I thought, this was supposed to be my dream not a bloody nightmare.

I was getting very angry at the way things were turning out, but then again what good will that do me. I must have sat for a good hour before dragging myself up and starting off again.

I found myself going through a very thick part of the forest. I don't think we came this way, because Fatso would not been able to get through here. It was too thick.

I am lost now, good and proper. I am not even going to attempt to try and get through this, I have no chance. I must go back to where I sat down and start again from there. I don't remember looking from where I had come from before starting out this morning, I was in a daze.

I found it difficult to turn back. I did not want to use the time up or the energy. I wanted to keep going forward and on to the cabin, but at the same time I have to be logical. I am going nowhere fast in this thick part of the woods, so turn back I did.

It took about one and a half hours to get back to where I had rested earlier. That was a waste of time and energy, I must take more notice before starting out. Looking back, then forward, I could see that I had veered to my right at about forty five degrees, putting me into the thick wood.

I sat down again and thought, to hell with it, I will stay here tonight, what a waste of a day.

No, you will not! There is still about three hours of

daylight left. You can have fifteen minutes then you can set off again. You called Fatso a fat lazy sod; how about you then? Yes, that's right. Stick to the routine like you should and you will have a better chance that way.

I was just walking now, there was no admiring the trees or the scenery and all I can think about is getting back to the nice warm cabin.

It will not be warm in the cabin now; I had put the fire out before I left. Even if I had not, it would not be alight now, or I should say when I get there, if I get there. Having said that the cabin will be warmer than out here,

I used about two of the three hours of daylight up, by which time I was totally exhausted.

I should light a fire, I am very, very cold now. But as I said earlier, finding the wood was very difficult or it certainly seemed that way. I did make an effort, a big effort and gathered some wood for the fire. Searching in the snow for bits of twigs, which were all I could find. It made a small but effective fire, it not only took the chill off but it cheered me up a little.

Sleep came and went in fits and starts. Some very deep and some just cat naps, (I think). I was thinking this is no good; I will have to try and get back into the two hours waking up at a time routine.

I wondered what happened to it. Am I letting go?

Is it the severe cold? Or exhaustion? I do not know anymore and I am beginning not to care. The days were just melted into one, I don't know how long it's been since I lost Fatso, but it seemed a long time ago now.

Before setting off the next day I had a block of chocolate for my breakfast, the last block. That was the last of my food, this is not going to get any easier. I suppose it's one way to lose weight. (That's not very funny I thought.)

I know now, that my situation is somewhat desperate.

I just walked and walked, I do not want to play this game anymore. I just want to be with Nadine, nice and warm, in bed making love.

Even having a drink with the cast out of *Blazing Saddles*, in that pub I stopped at on the way here.

Anything would be better than this shit.

I did not give a toss what time it was, or if I was making good time any more, I do not even or know or care which direction I am going in.

Now and again I would pull myself together and throw my shoulders back and try and keep control of things, it's not easy now.

I was struggling along when I tripped on something under the snow, a rock maybe, a fallen tree, I don't know what it was. Whatever the bloody thing was I rolled down an embankment.

This time as I laid in the snow I was not laughing, not like the time it happened with Fatso, and even that turned out not to be funny. This time I did not want to get up. This time it hurt. This time it took a lot out of me. I think I will just give up, lay here and wait for the end.

Maybe they are looking for me right now. Maybe if I lay here, someone will find me and take me back to the cabin, where they will have a big roaring fire on the go, with a mug of sweet coffee made just for me. Now that would be wonderful. If they did that for me, I would take them all to dinner at the Arc-en-Ciel. We could all have a lovely meal and plenty of wine and sit by a big fire afterwards.

I don't know how long I was lying there, I even thought of the two carpets again. When I came to my senses I was very disappointed that I was not in the Arc-en-Ciel with Nadine, Mike and Joe, and that big roaring fire.

By now I was shivering and chilled to the bone. I have to get myself up and moving, or I will freeze to death.

This is decision time.

Nobody is looking for me, and even if they are, there is not much chance that they will find me. They will have no idea where I am.

The thought of death struck a chord. I did not like the way I was behaving. I thought, I am letting go now, and this will not do.

I picked myself up, adjusted my clothing, found my rifle, took a big breath and started walking.

Look at your watch, do forty-five, stick to the plan and show what you are made of. After all you are an Englishman, it's a stiff upper lip and get on with it. That's how England built its empire. Stop feeling sorry for you, you big tart.

I did a lot better that day, better than could have been expected. After all I had nearly given up that morning. If I can pull myself out of these dark periods then there is still hope for me.

That night went fast, so fast I do not remember settling down.

Waking up the next day I thought, Christ, I'm hungry. What the hell am I going to do about food?

Try not to think too much of it, just get on your way.

I will stop thinking about it, but someone should tell my stomach to stop thinking about it, it is starting to hurt.

I had done about two hours, when I felt a feeling I had

not experienced before. Something inside warned me be alert, danger about. I stopped and looked all around for a minute or so, but saw nothing. I have no idea what it was but there was something.

I walked past a thick clump of big trees and there in my path was a big black bear.

It's times like this I wish I could be religious and ask for a helping hand, but I am not, so I will have to think of something else.

The bear was eating something, but stopped when I appeared. It looked up at me like a dog when it has a bone, not wanting to let go of the meal, but wanting to keep an eye on me at the same time.

I just stood there looking at him, not wanting to move, and at the same time wanting to run like hell; my heart was pumping like a piston.

They say when you meet a bear like this, you should roll up into a ball and let it play with you until it gets tired of it. We'll let me tell you, I've no intention of trying that theory out, that's a lot easier said than done. You would need more nerve then I.

We looked at each other for what seemed a bloody long time.

He obviously took me as a threat to his meal.

He stood up on his hind legs and started to roar.

He was about seven feet tall if he was an inch.

'Right, it's you or me,' I said, kidding myself.

I slid the rifle off my shoulder and cocked it ready for firing. This I found very difficult, as my fingers were numb now.

He didn't come at me at first, he just stood there roaring

his protest at my presence, I think this was his way of showing how hard he was. Well he convinced me.

Okay I thought, if you don't want to hurt me I will not hurt you. So the best thing to do I thought was to fire the rifle into the air and see what happens.

This I did, what a bloody noise, it even made me jump.

This bear had obviously never heard a rifle before, and he was impressed enough. He was off faster than the one I saw catching the deer, I felt like sinking to my knees with relief but I did not want to hang around here.

Thank goodness for that, I was not hurt and neither was he. Now I will have to get going from here before he comes back for his dinner.

Walking past his dinner I could see there was still plenty of good meat on it, so I hurriedly took out my knife and cut off a big chunk. It was still warm. I hope he does not mind, but I will not be hanging around to find out.

Time means little or nothing now. Having said that, I do try and look at my watch regularly. How regular this is I do not know, as I can just about see the dial now. I keep telling myself, stick to the routine.

All I do now is stop when I am tired, sleep when I think I should, but right now I am hungry, so I will have my share of the bear's spoils. I gathered in some twigs, cleared a piece of ground ready to light a fire. This I was looking forward to very much.

Arranging the twigs and placing some pages from a note book I had on me in the middle, now it was ready for lighting. This piece of meat would be like a Sunday roast to me.

Reaching into my pocket for the disposable lighter I have

been using all the time out here, I could not find it. It must be in the other pocket I thought. Having looked, it was not there either.

I began to panic now, where the hell is it.

I turned every pocket I had inside out. It had gone.

Christ, when was the last time I used it? I was always careful to put it away when I had finished with it.

I even looked into the lining of my coat, still no bloody lighter. Where did it get to? The only thing that I can think of, I must have lost the damn thing when I took that tumble yesterday, or the day before that, or whenever it was.

That's all I need now. All that bloody hard

work looking for wood, then having nothing to light it with.

I've never eaten raw meat before and I do not think I can now. I suppose I could rub two sticks together but I have not got the energy to waste. I decided to go to sleep and hope to forget about my hunger. I did go to sleep, but with the exhaustion not for long. Feeling the hunger I could not sleep for any length of time.

Right, I am going to do what has to be done.

First I will eat this piece of raw meat. That should give me some energy, and satisfy my hunger for a little while at least. Then I hope to get some decent sleep, so when I wake in the morning I should be in a fair state to carry on.

I started to nibble the meat, a little at a time. It turned my stomach at first, but I was determined to eat the lot and before I had realised, I was taking bloody big chunks from it. When I had finished my stomach was full and I must say it hurt a bit, but at the same time it felt comforting. It also seemed to warm me up.

It did not take long to get to sleep this time, and I slept well, not like the first part of the night.

The next morning was just like the last five or six. When I awoke I was bloody freezing. I find if I can keep out of the wind it's not half as cold, but it's still bad enough. It is really getting to me now, I hope I can hold out, just keep going, do not give up and there's a chance for me. There is always a chance I try to convince myself.

Talk's cheap, yes. So you are not as fit as you thought are you, big head?

I kept going that day but I don't think I got very far. My body is aching from top to bottom, and my toes and fingers I can hardly feel at times. Maybe I'm getting frost bite, please don't let that happen, that will finish me off.

I soon got hungry but there is nothing at the moment I can do about it. I really must try and think of something else.

I bedded down early that night, but it was much the same as the first part of last night. Sleep for thirty minutes, wake up freezing and sleep for thirty minutes. I still keep dreaming of the two carpets and I can't figure out why. As I said, it must be a psychological feeling of being warm.

The following morning when I awoke, I was really chilled to the bone more than ever before and didn't want to move.

Come on now, you know if you can get walking it will warm you up, it will be for the best.

No, I can't go any further. I'm too bloody cold and tired. My legs hardly work now in the morning.

I was having this little argument with myself when it struck me.

Christ, that's it! The two bloody carpets.

That's what they are trying to tell me, what a thick sod I've been. The sun was setting in the west, so the direction of the orange carpet is east/west. The direction of the red carpet is north/south.

Well, that's the spur I needed very badly, I had just about given up.

I was soon on my feet looking up at the sun which was just on the rise. I was quite excited now. If I travel due south I should come across the lake I camped by. The lake where I threw the snowball at Fatso's arse. If I do hit the lake it should be easy enough to find my bearings as I then turn west. That should bring me to the river I followed from the cabin.

Yes! There is hope. I've got a good chance now.

The sun was coming up on my left, so I faced ninety degrees to its position and set off walking. All that day my hopes were very high. I did not even think too much about being hungry. I would have a mouthful of snow from time to time and it tasted good.

Don't have too much I told myself. I have read, eating too much snow will lower my temperature and that I can't afford to do.

Other than the hunger, this is the best I have felt for, oh, it must be a week now.

The walking did warm me up, but it also knackered me. As I said, walking in this shit was like walking on a water bed. It's the warmth that counts at this stage. I only wish that I could get a fire going somehow, or the sun would give off some heat but there is little chance of that at this time of year.

It was about two in the afternoon when a horrible thought hit me,

What if I have already passed the lake?

I have no way of knowing, please don't let that happen.

At around four I sat down to have a rest as the sun was going down. While I sat my hopes went from sky-high, down to just about zero, I was feeling very sorry again for myself now.

Sitting here thinking, I have decided what I must do. It is to give it one more day going south, then take stock and plan my next move. It's not looking half as good as it did this morning, when I had thought of the two carpets.

If necessary I will summon up the strength and climb up a tree to find some sort of bearing. Maybe I can see the lake from a height or the big hill on the other side of the cabin.

While I sat trying to work out the best thing to do, looking through the trees I noticed a flat area, of what looked like an ice covered piece of land.

I guess it must have been no more than fifty yards away, I can't really tell in this light. I should walk along that, with it being flat. It will make going a lot easier I said to myself. I made my way towards it through the trees.

When I reached the tree line, much to my surprise it turned out to be the lake.

It took my breath away. I felt the emotion well up inside me. I even found myself crying with relief. Two fantastic bits of luck in one day. I have never had two bits of luck in my life, never mind in one day.

I don't know how long I stood there looking around just pleased that I had found the lake.

Anyway, after I pulled myself together, I started walking in the direction of the cabin.

I hope very much that tonight will be the bloody last one spent out here. The cold has just about seen me off, I think it's only been dogged determination that has seen me this far.

As I walked my mind was on the cabin, Nadine and a warm meal by a big fire.

I was somewhat taken aback when I saw some dog tracks in the snow. They must have been looking for me with the dogs, I thought! There were several tracks. Maybe two or three dogs, or more. It really does look as though I've made it. It can't be that far to the cabin now.

I had better rest somewhere here and get an early start tomorrow. I looked up to pick out a spot to bed down for the night by the trees.

There were the three dogs, maybe four, I cannot see that well now, but no one was with them.

'Am I glad to see you, where are your handlers?'

I started to walk towards them and it was then I came to my senses. Rubbing my eyes to get a better view, that was the moment I realised, they were not dogs.

Yes, you have guessed it, they were three of the biggest wolves I have seen.

I stopped in my tracks, slid the rifle off my shoulder and took aim. I could hardly see them now, my eyes are that bad. Anyway I fired off a shot that sent them running into the forest.

I had better walk a bit further along the lake, and put some distance between them and me. I will not be bedding down here tonight. Even going a few hundred yards down the lake side will be better than nothing, I was thinking.

I realised with mistaking the wolves for dogs that I was not fully alert so to freshen up I pushed my big heavy hood off my face to the back of my neck for some fresh air.

I had only walked a few yards when I was hit from behind and sent sprawling to the ground face first. I had no idea what had hit me till I heard the snarling of the wolf on my back, tearing at the hood I had just pushed back. It was pulling so hard I thought it was going to choke me.

The three had crept up from behind me, after they had got over the noise of the shot. One had my hood, one had hold of my boot and the third had my left forearm in his jaws.

I was on the verge of passing out, when I took off my right mitten with my teeth and reached for the trigger of the rifle.

It took all my strength and for a moment I did not think I would make it, but make it I did and I pulled the trigger. The noise sounded good to me, and it did the trick.

The wolves jumped back with shock for a few seconds and this was enough time for me to roll away, taking the rifle with me. Where I found the strength, I do not know.

I knelt on one knee and fired off all five bullets at them, and one by one they fell to the ground. I will have no more trouble from those bastards, they are all dead now.

It must have been at least five or six minutes before I dared to move. I just knelt there looking at them, waiting for them to stir.

As I knelt I felt my left arm getting warmer, and the pain getting worse. I took off my parka, rolled up my left sleeve to have a look. Sure enough there were deep puncture marks in my arm.

After cleaning my wound with snow, which also cooled it down, it made it feel a lot better than I think it is. I wrapped my handkerchief around it to stop the bleeding.

Come on, I said to myself, get on your way it should not be long now. One more night and you should be safe and sound in the cabin; all it will take is one final effort.

I started to walk. My mind is in turmoil, thinking of what had happened and what could have happened to me, back there with the wolves. I know I was lucky to get away with my life. I kept looking around to make sure there were no more following me. I think they must have sensed I was very weak, and that's why they attacked me. Putting my hood back when I did surely saved my life; how lucky I was.

I walked and walked not wanting to stop, in fear that there were more of them behind me. I reloaded the rifle just in case. I did not even stop to do that, even though it was very difficult with my numb fingers.

It took some time before I noticed that I was limping. Has that bloody wolf done some damage to my leg or foot?

Looking down and feeling my leg for any damage I was relieved to find that the only damage was to the heel of my boot. There was a big chunk missing. Well that's a blessing, I can live with that for now.

I don't remember stopping for my fifteen minutes rest. I don't think I did stop, I didn't want to stop. I think it was fear that drove me on. I know this is a stupid thing to do, but it seemed as though I had no control over my actions now.Something was driving me on and on and I kept on walking and walking.

It's light now. I didn't even notice the sun coming up.

I stopped to look around. Am I hallucinating, or do the surroundings look familiar? Am I somewhere near the cabin? Or is it wishful thinking?

In front of me was a slight incline, about forty feet long, rising up about ten feet. I crawled up what to me seemed like a mountain, on all fours. When I reached the ridge and looked over, there it was.

To you it looks like a log cabin. To me it looks like Heaven, Utopia, and Salvation.

I must be hallucinating, there's smoke coming from the cabin chimney.

I only hope I am not hallucinating about the cabin. I dropped the rifle, tried to get up, but my strength had all gone. I tried again to get to my feet but the effort took its toll and I fell back into the snow.

I thought, so near yet so far, surely I can make it now. After getting through all that, I cannot fail now. But it wasn't to be. It was then I blacked out.

I felt myself coming to, I also felt quite warm. Am I in Heaven? No, they don't take atheists into Heaven do they? I don't want to open my eyes just in case I was in that other place. It would only be what I deserved.

Anyway, I did open my eyes.

There, looking over me was the ugliest angel I have ever seen. Not that I have seen any angels. It was big Mike.

'Christ, Mike, you might be ugly but am I so glad to see you.

I felt the emotion well up and my eyes filled.

'Hold on, you are safe now,' Mike said.

'How did I get down here?'

'I carried you from the top of the small ridge, just east of the cabin. I came out of the cabin to take a leak. It was then I saw something lying up there.

At first I thought it was a wolf watching me so I got out my rifle and I was just about to take a shot when I realised it had not moved. I took a closer look, and there you were sunning yourself.

You have had a disagreement with something. Your back is ripped to shreds. There's also a half inch deep gash in the back of your neck, not to mention your left arm.

'Is it still there?' I asked.

'Yes, you have been very lucky.'

I feel as stiff as a board and I am aching all over and so bloody hungry. I could eat a scabby cow between two well pissed mattresses. I tried to sit up, it was then I felt everything hurt.

'You stay where you are,' Mike said. 'I will feed you some soup.'

'Have I been asleep all night, Mike?'

'No, you have been asleep for three nights. This is your fourth day,' he said.

'You're joking, Mike!'

'No, I am not. Here get this soup down you.'

I tried to sit up but could not find the strength.

Mike helped me up and held me like a baby.

The soup tasted magic, I could feel the warmth of it going all the way to my stomach. I could only manage four or five spoonfuls I was that tired.

'Mike, that's the best soup I have ever tasted.'

'You should try my curry,' he said proudly.

'Maybe, when I am a bit fitter I will.'

'You rest now,' he said. 'I will wake you later and give you some more soup. Sometime later in the day I would like to get you out of bed to do some walking.'

'You must be taking the piss. I don't want to walk ever again.'

'No, you will need some exercise to get your muscles working. Now get some sleep and stop talking, I want to get you into hospital as soon as possible.'

I did manage a few more spoonfuls of the soup. As you can imagine I slept pretty damn good, knowing I was safe, warm and with some of Mike's homemade soup inside me, I felt better than I have for some time.

I woke up naturally sometime later that day, I'd say around five in the evening.

'Mike! How about some of that nectar you call soup.'

'Coming right up, you lazy dog.'

Again I tried to get up. I did manage to get so far but my body ached all over, I have never felt so sore.

'Did you give me a good punching while I was asleep?' I asked Mike.

'No, but something did while you were out there. What happened?'

'Oh, not much. I was attacked by three wolves, that's all. Nothing special.'

'Just three? Are you sure you just had a fight with them and nothing else?'

'You don't think I shagged them do you? Don't make me laugh, it hurts too much,' I replied. 'By the way, what happened to the other horse, Mike?'

'Oh, I turned him loose when I got here five days ago, he will make his own way back. I would have come looking for you then but there were no tracks to follow. It must have snowed after you left the cabin.

'Yes, it did,' I grunted. I could just about talk.

'Come to think of it, Mike, what are you doing here? I thought you had a new job to go to.'

'I had, but when I got there the materials had not turned up, I was informed it would be another month or so before they would arrive. I said to myself, another month! I might as well spend it at the cabin with you.'

'That was bloody lucky for me,' I said, 'otherwise I would most probably be dead by now.'

I finished the bowl of soup by myself with a little effort and was just about to lie down.

'No, you don't, come on, out of there and walk round the cabin a couple of times; I will give you a hand.'

'Behave Mike, I can't possibly do that.'

With that, Mike picked me up bodily and put my feet on the floor.

'Listen you big ape, let me get some sleep.'

'You have slept for four days. Now it's time for work.'

'Right,' I said. 'I will do three laps of the cabin and that's all.'

'You are in no fit state to be telling me what you will do and not do,' said big Mike.

When I had done the three laps with Mike holding on to me, I could not get into bed quick enough.

'Mike, I don't think I will be ready tomorrow, I am feeling so weak.'

Mike looked at me in a serious manner and said, 'I must get you back for expert treatment.

I have cleaned all your wounds the best I can, but they need more. You will most probably need injections of antibiotics. And things I can't give you here, so don't argue. You are going to hospital tomorrow even if I have to tie you onto the back of my skidoo. So eat and drink as much as you can, save your strength, get a good night's sleep and it will be easier for you.'

Next morning when I awoke, I felt very relaxed mentally, but still very stiff and sore. The fire was burning and there was a lovely smell of coffee.

Mike came in from outside with some more logs for the fire.

'Oh, you are awake, good for you. I have got some breakfast ready, would you like some?'

'What is it?' I asked. 'Christ, what am I saying? It does not matter what it is, just give me a plateful.

'Can you get out of bed by yourself?'

'I don't think so Mike, but I will have a go this morning, just for you.'

I managed to get halfway out and Mike helped me with the other half.

'Okay Mike,' I said. 'Let me try and walk myself.

I took a few doddery steps to the table and sat down.

'How about that then, Mike?'

'Very good, get this down you and I will take you outside for a walk around the cabin.'

'I think that will be a bit too much for me.'

'Too much or not, we will give it a go.'

'What's this, "we will give it a go" shit? You can walk all right, and it's me that's giving it a go.'

'Oh shut the hell up moaning and get your breakfast.'

'That's right, pick on an old cripple,' I grumbled.

At that we both started to laugh; laughing hurt me too much.

'Look,' he said. 'After your breakfast, walk around the cabin. Just a couple of times, that's all, to get your muscles working, then get back into bed. I would like to set off at about eleven, eleven thirty, when the sun is up and warm. It should take about three hours to get you into town.'

'Three hours!' I said. 'It took me about three days. How fast can your skidoo go?'

'It has a top speed of ninety miles an hour. We will do around seventy all the way back because all I have to do is follow my own tracks. It should be quite easy.'

'All right, Mike, you know best.'

'Oh, at last. A bit of recognition.' He smiled.

When I had finished my breakfast I took a big breath, stood up and made for the door, very slowly.

'Do you want any help?' Mike asked.

'Yes, any chance of you carrying me around the outside of the cabin twice?'

'Very funny, get on with it.'

Stepping outside the fresh air felt wonderful, cold and fresh on my face. It livened me up no end, and I do feel I am a lot stronger. I walked very slowly, it must have taken me an hour but I did it. But as I got to the cabin door, the last few yards were too much.

'Mike. Can you give me a hand on the home straight?'

'No problem, big boy, you did well. Have your well-earned rest now. I will wake you when I am ready for the off.'

Going back into the cabin it felt like the first night I

had stayed there, after coming down off the hill where I had stayed just too long and got a little chilly. The warmth greeted me like an old friend, but it felt a lot better this time. I flopped onto the bed and covered myself up and let Mike get on with getting things ready. I was soon asleep.

Mike woke me with a gentle shaking of my shoulder.

'Are you ready, buddy?'

'Not really, Mike. Is there any chance of a couple of days' sleep before we set off.' I smirked.

'No, don't even think of going back to sleep.'

'Okay, it's no good putting it off, let's get to it.'

'I have a spare skidoo suit for you. It will keep you warm and also keep the wind out on the journey home. Come on, I will help you.'

'Mike, how I can ever thank you? You saved my life and then you have looked after me like a brother'

'I will think of something,' he said with that big daft smile.

Everything was there outside the door, ready.

'Can you walk to the skidoo?'

'Yes, but you will have to give me a helping hand to get on.'

'I intended to do just that, come on, then wagons roll.'

I got to the skidoo all right but that was it.

'Okay, Mike, Where do you want me?'

'Just wait there a minute, I will get it started.'

This he did with no bother.

'Right,' he said, 'let me put you on the back.'

After doing this, he slid in front of me.

'Put this belt around you and pass it to me.'

This I did with great difficulty, Mike tied us both together, laughing.

'And this is just in case you decide to go sunning yourself again.'

'I suppose you think that's very funny.'

'Does it feel comfortable?' he asked.

'Spot on,' I replied.

'Good, then it's off we go.'

Mike revved up and pulled away slowly.

'I will take it easy to start with. If you have any problems let me know right away.'

'If I do have any problems you will be the first to know, don't worry about that.'

It felt good in this skidoo suit, nice and warm, and with a big pair of mittens on I was snug as a bug in a rug. I put my arms around Mike, well almost round, rested my head on his broad shoulders, and guess what? Yes, that's right, I fell asleep.

I felt the skidoo come to a stop.

'Are we there already I asked?'

'No. We have done one and a half hours and I have stopped for a hot mug of coffee.'

Mike undid the belt. 'If I take you off do you think you can stand?' he asked.

'Let's give it a go,' I said.

Mike got off, and then lifted me off. I could stand, but just about.

'Lean me on that tree, I should be okay there.'

Mike poured the coffee. 'Here be careful, it's very hot,' he said.

He was not kidding but I managed to finish the full mug.

'How long are we staying, Mike?'

'Why, do you want to get going?'

'I think it would be best, I am getting weak again.'

'Come on then, on you get. We should be in town within two hours, then you can forget all about this.

'No,' I said, 'that's the last thing I want to do. I will never forget what has happened to me out here. Never.'

He nodded, as if to agree.

This time when we set off things were so different. As soon as I sat on the skidoo I could feel every movement, even the engine ticking over. This part of the journey was not going to be any picnic.

Mike set off and before we had done ten yards I was starting to hurt. Every little bump, every little jerk hurt like hell. But I was not going to tell Mike, he would have just stopped every hundred yards or so and then it would have taken all day to get back. I clung on the best I could not wanting Mike to think I was hurting and in some pain.

We had done about one hour and my body was racked with pain. I did think of asking Mike to go faster, but that would given the game away.

The next thing I knew, Mike and two medics were putting me onto a stretcher.

'Christ, Mike,' I said. 'That last part hurt.'

'Yes, I know,' he replied.

'How could you possibly know?' I asked.

'Well every time it hurt you, you nearly squeezed the life out of me, so I thought if it's going to hurt at seventy miles an hour it might as well hurt at eighty miles an hour. So I opened up a little and got here in one and a half hours.'

'I suppose that makes sense, but I am glad that's over with. I'm looking forward to getting into bed now.'

'That will not be too long, you are on your way there now, it will be about two minutes. Just take things steady.'

Next morning when the doctor came to see me he informed me that I was a very lucky man indeed.

'How do you mean?' I asked.

'Well for a start, I don't know how you did not bleed to death. It must have been the cold temperature that helped to keep you alive. A lot of your wounds had turned septic, plus you must have lost half of your body weight. Just what did happen to you?'

'I went for a long walk,' I said jokingly.

'It must have been some walk.'

'How long do you think I will be in here for, Doctor?'

'Oh, with a bit of luck no more than a week. We have treated your wounds. At one time I thought I was in sewing class. Your back is like a patchwork quilt now. You will need to take antibiotics for a week to ten days and that should clear up the infection.

'The wound on the back of your neck is the worst, how the hell did you get that?'

'Do not ask,' I replied.

I had a comfortable night.

Next morning after the doctor's round, the nurse gave me a good breakfast. I did not eat it all, but what I did eat, I really enjoyed. I was still very sore, but somehow I knew that the worst was over, I was so thankful for that. All I need now is a few days in bed, some good food and I will be as right as rain.

Later that day Nadine came to see me. I was dozing when she walked in.

I heard her say to the nurse, 'I will not wake him. Would you tell him when he wakes up, that Nadine called to see him, please?'

'Tell me yourself', I said, trying to sit up.

Nadine walked over to the bed.

'Bonjour,' she said softly.

'How lovely to see you. There were times out there when I thought I would never see you again.'

'Well, you are out of my sight for just three weeks and look what happens to you.'

'That was a quick change of mood,' I quipped. 'Anyway, I've got to enjoy my holidays while I can, I can't rely on anyone else.'

'Very funny,' she said. She was not amused.

'I was only trying to make light of it, Nadine. Do not be mad at me. I've had enough of the dark side of life in the last three weeks, and I did think of you, often.'

'Yes I bet you did.'

'Truly I did. How did you know I was here?'

'Your friend Mike told Joe and he told me.'

'Anyway, I am so glad to see you, Nadine, you have made my day. Have you been here long?'

She smiled. 'You are a smooth so and so, you know how long I have been here. But how can I be mad at you for long, I have missed you so much and at one stage I thought you were not coming back.'

'That's better,' I said, with a twinkle in my eye. I just can't help myself.

She asked, 'How long will you be in for?'

'The doctor told me about a week, all being well.'

'I will come every day to see you.'

'You better had or there will be trouble.'

'You are in no fit state to threaten me,' Nadine said, with a big smile.

'No, but I should be in a weeks' time.'

'You are all talk,' she replied. 'Is there anything I can bring you?'

'Yes,' I said. 'Would you bring me some chocolate and some peanuts, please?'

'That should be no problem. How about a big tub of ice-cream?' she asked.

'Ice cream? Ice cream? You must be bloody joking. I never want to see ice ever again.'

'Okay,' she said, 'keep your hair on. I will see you tomorrow just after lunch.'

'Thanks again for coming to see me, it was wonderful seeing you. It has bucked me up no end.'

'What do you mean? Bucked you up?'

'Oh. I will explain some other time.'

Nadine kissed me on the cheeks. That felt good.

'Goodbye for now, and there's a lot more where that came from.'

'I am looking forward to receiving them.'

That week in the hospital went fairly quickly, with everyone making a fuss over me, which I did enjoy. It's not often I am fussed over. What with Nadine visiting every day, and Mike and Joe calling in on me a couple of times during my stay, it all helped to pass the time.

The first time Joe called to see me, I could not apologise enough about losing his horse and saddle.

'Do not worry about it. We will sort things out when you are better.'

Although, I did have a few flashbacks of the events that had occurred back there in the wild. They kept going around and around in my head.

But I have now decided to try and put them to the back of my mind.

While in the hospital all I did was eat and sleep, I was putting on weight fast. Oh, I did take some light exercise to keep my arms and legs in use.

On the following Thursday morning at ten thirty the doctor came to see me.

'Well,' he said, 'you have done remarkably well in a week. You have put back some of the lost weight, had plenty of rest and a little bit of exercise. So providing you have somewhere to stay you can leave today.'

'That sounds all right to me,' I said. 'I suppose you will be glad to see the back of me.'

'Not really, you have done as you were told, and I think some of the nurses have taken a shine to you. It must be that English accent of yours.'

'Well, it can't be my good looks at the moment can it? You and your staff have treated me like a prince, I can't thank you enough.'

'It was a good thing you had your blue cross medical insurance,' he stressed, 'or this would have cost you a small fortune. Well, do you have anywhere to go?'

'Just let me make a phone call.'

'You're not under arrest,' he said with a grin.

'You know what I mean,' I told him.

'Okay, let my staff know what you have decided and they will inform me.'

He shook my hand and wished me good luck.

'Again, thank you very much for your care and attention. Maybe I can buy you dinner one of the nights soon.'

'I will take you up on that,' he said.

'I hope so,' I replied.

I phoned the motel and asked for Nadine

'Hello Nadine, how you are this fine day?'

'Never mind me, how are you? I will be in later today to see you.'

'That's what I am calling you about. The doctor said if I have anywhere to stay I can leave the hospital today. So, is there any chance of a room at the motel for a week or so?'

'No,' came the reply.

'Why, are you full?' I asked, feeling very disappointed.

'No,' she said again, 'you will be staying at my place until you can look after yourself.'

'That may take some time.'

'That's what I am hoping,' she said. 'I have a few things to do, but I will be there to pick you up at three o'clock. How does that sound?'

'I will be ready and waiting for you, it can't come fast enough for me. See you then.'

Nadine walked into my room at spot on three with a big smile on her face from ear to ear.

'Well, that's a happy face, have you won the lottery?' I asked. 'How nice to see you, Nadine.

I'm all set to go, I just want to thank the nurses then we can get on our way.'

I was still a bit unsteady on my feet but a whole lot better than a week ago.

Walking into the nurses' rest room I was given a standing ovation.

'Behave yourselves; it's I who should be giving you an ovation. I have come to thank you for everything. You have all been wonderful. I hope to have a party next week and you are all welcome to come, I will let you know when and where. Thanks again and bye for now.'

One by one they came over to me and gave me a hug and told me to stay out of trouble.

'I will for the next few weeks at least.'

Nadine and I walked down the long corridor. She carried my bag and I carried me. I was a lot better now; walking is not all that difficult. The little exercise I had been doing in my room has done the trick.

Driving to Nadine's house and seeing all that snow and the icicles hanging off the houses brought back the trip , but I just shrugged and sat back to enjoy the ride.

'Why did you shrug your shoulders like that?' Nadine asked.

'Oh, I was just thinking of my trip to Mike's cabin.'

'I will help you forget about that,' she smiled.

'What do you have in mind? Don't you forget I am not one hundred per cent fit.'

'Don't you worry about that, I will do all the work.'

We both burst out laughing. It really felt good to laugh again, it seems such a long time since I had.

Driving up that lovely driveway to Cotero, seeing the trees in their splendour was a wonderful sight. When the car turned around the bend my heart was filled with joy. Walking into the house, the smell of pine filled my nostrils. It was a far better smell then the hospital; then again any smell is better than the hospital.

'Would you like anything to eat or drink?' Nadine asked me.

'No, thank you, they really did treat me well at the hospital.'

'How about getting into the jacuzzi?' she suggested.

'That's a brilliant idea. Will it take long to get ready?'

'No,' she replied, 'it is ready. All I have to do is turn on the bubbles. Come on, I will show you where it is and you can get in while I put your things away.'

This was some house, the jacuzzi is as big as my lounge back home,

Stripping off I noticed my back in the big mirrors on the changing room walls. It was like the doctor said, a bit of a mess. I slipped into the pool very slowly. At first it felt too hot, but just like getting in the bath I was soon used to it.

The jacuzzi was about ten feet in diameter and I would say four feet deep, with a seat all around it, maybe two feet down from the surface which I could sit on and just let the bubbles do their thing.

Now this did feel good, it should not take me long to get well with this sort of treatment.

It was not long before Nadine came in the room; she just had a big towel around her.

'This is really lovely, Nadine. Get yourself in.'

'That's just what I am going to do.'

She let the towel fall to the ground and revealed her gorgeous figure.

'I hope your intentions are honourable,' I said to her.

'We will have to wait and see, won't we,' she said with her lovely smile.

Nadine climbed into the pool on the opposite side to me, slowly, very slowly indeed.

'If I did not know better I would say you did that on purpose.'

'Moi, chéri?' came the reply.

'Oui, vous.'

It was not long before she was at my side.

'These bubbles feel so good, Nadine.

'Would you like me to turn them up a little?' she asked.

'Just a little,' I replied.

'She stood on the seat and leaned over to a valve on the side of the pool.

'With her lovely buttock facing me, I could not resist, I just had to kiss it. She let out a yelp which made us both laugh.

'I think your intentions are not honourable,' she said smiling. 'Are the bubbles strong enough for you ?'

'Yes thank you, they are very soothing. They are doing my back the world of good.'

Nadine sat down again next to me this time. We just sat silently for a few minutes enjoying the heat and the bubbles.

The next thing I knew Nadine had put her hand on my thigh.

'Oh, and what are you up to now?'

'Just relax and I will help to make you feel better,' she murmured.

'How are you going to do that?' I said, grinning from ear to ear like the big kid I am.

'By the look on your face I think you already know.'

'All I can say is, be gentle with me, or I might just struggle.'

'You? Struggle? I don't think so.'

'Well I might, I have my reputation to think of. I do not want all the girls to think I am easy.'

Nadine snuggled up and kissed me fully on the lips.

I felt myself getting aroused and took her in my arms. She was gentle with me and I forgot all about my injuries for a while. We were in the jacuzzi for at least thirty minutes.

'I hope that was not too much of an ordeal for you,' she said.

'Well, let me put it this way. I will not report you to the police this time.'

We climbed out of the pool and into the shower.

After the shower she asked, 'Could you eat something now?'

'Yes, I think I could now. What would you suggest?'

'You can have anything you like.'

'Was I that good?'

'No, but I was,' she said laughing.

'Go on then, I fancy a ham salad sandwich washed down with a cup of red rose tea.'

'Go and sit in the lounge. I will bring it to you and you can relax for real now.'

'You say that now, but I do not trust you anymore.'

'Go on, get in there and stop talking silly.'

'You are the boss.'

After our snack we just sat looking into the log fire. The next thing I know I am waking up; I had fallen into a lovely deep sleep.

'So you are still with us,' Nadine said, smiling.

'Well that was a nice little nap,' I replied.

'What would you like to do now?' she asked.

'What time is it please?'

'It's eight thirty. Would you like to watch some TV?'

'Not really. But there is nothing else I can think of.'

Nadine smiled and replied, 'I can think of something.'

'No! No! No! I am knackered as it is, are you trying to kill me off?'

'I am only fooling with you,' she said. 'How about a nice bottle of wine to finish off the day?'

'I would not mind that at all.'

I woke up next morning feeling quite refreshed. I leaned over and kissed Nadine on her cheek.

'Bonjour ma chérie.'

'That was a nice alarm call,' she said, turning around to face me.

'How are you this fine morning?'

Nadine kissed me on my lips; the kiss must have lasted for ten minutes.

'Wow! That's a better alarm call than mine, it took my breath away.'

'Have you got your strength back?' she asked, looking me straight in my eyes.

'I know I should not say this, but yes. I have had a good night's sleep and I am ready for anything.'

'Anything?' she said, smiling.

'I hope I do not regret saying this, but yes, anything.'

'Why should you regret saying it?' she said as she snuggled up to me.

She felt soft and warm and I was not about to push her away.

We made love for most of the morning. After which she asked me what I would like to do today.

'Not a lot. I would like to have a dip in the jacuzzi first, and then I must go and see Joe and have a talk with him. I need to settle a few things between us.'

'Okay, when you have done that I will take you to lunch. Do you like Chinese food?'

'Yes I do, very much, I would like that.'

'I know a nice Chinese restaurant out of town. We will have a drive out there and spend the day away from here. How does that sound?'

'That's sounds wonderful, but would you run me into town first please, so I can talk to Joe?'

'Of course. While you are doing that I will look in at the motel to see that things are going okay.'

'Come on then, get yourself in the jacuzzi, then get dressed, and we can get away.'

We drew up at the motel at around one fifteen. After parking the car, Nadine made her way into the motel and I walked across the road to Joe's garage.

I went around the back. As I did I shouted, 'Bonjour, Monsieur Weall.'

A boy of about sixteen appeared.

'Bonjour,' I said to him. 'Ou est Monsieur Weall, s'il vous plaît?'

'L' Arc-en-Ciel,' came the reply.

'Merci.' I might have guessed, after all it is lunch time.

I walked over to the Arc-en-Ciel. I knew which room he would be in; the bar of course.

'Bonjour, Joe.'

'Bonjour, mon ami, it is so good to see you,' he said in that deep voice of his.

'I have come to settle things with you, Joe.'

'Have a drink first, then we talk.'

'I will, if I can buy you and your friends a round.'

'Mai oui, that's very nice of you.'

'Not at all, it will be my pleasure. What would you all like to drink?'

'Just a beer,' they answered at once.

Halfway down our drink I asked Joe, 'How much do I owe you for the horse?'

'Nothing, my friend, he had just about had his day and he had served me well.'

'Please, let me pay something. After all is said and done, it was me who lost him.'

'No, it was not your fault, my friend, the weather caught you out. It has done it to more experienced men than you. Okay, fifty dollars,' he sighed.

'Fifty dollars! I said. 'No, he must have been worth more.'

'Give me fifty dollars, and that will be it settled.'

'Okay, if that suits you, its suits me, and thanks again.'

'No thanks necessary. I am happy that you got back safe and now looking a lot better than you looked last week.'

'I feel a lot better, merci.'

'Nadine is looking after you then, yes?'

'Oh yes, very well indeed.'

'Stay and have a few drinks with us?' Joe asked.

'I will, some other day, but Nadine is taking me to lunch shortly.'

'You two are getting on very well together. You are very lucky, yes?

'Yes I am. I will finish this drink and I will be off to meet her.'

After emptying my glass I thanked Joe again.

'That's okay, we must have another drink sometime.'

'Of course. I am having a party next Friday night and you and your friends are most welcome to join in.'

'I will be there,' he said with a broad grin. 'Just tell me where and what time is it starting?'

'Well, it is going to be here in the restaurant, let's say eight o'clock. We can have a few drinks at the bar, and then I will buy dinner for everyone who turns up.

'Right,' said Joe. See you maybe tonight. You have a nice day.'

I walked very slowly back to the motel, Nadine was in the reception, waiting.

'Is everything okay then?' I asked.

'Yes, no problems at all, we can get on our way now.'

'Is it far?'

'About a thirty-five minute drive. Why, are you tired now?'

'Just a little, but I can rest in the car on the way. Don't worry, I will be all right, let's go.'

It was warm in the car, I had not noticed how cold it was while walking down the street.

I reclined the back of my seat and just relaxed on the way there. The trees had snow on the leaves. I still think they look lovely, but I am glad I am not out there at the cabin. The temperature is still well below freezing.

'Here we are,' Nadine said. 'That went fast enough, did it not?'

'I must have dozed off, it looks a very nice place.'

Walking into the entrance, a smartly dressed waiter asked, 'Table for two, sir?'

'Yes, please,' I replied.

He showed us to the table near the far window. To get to

the table we had to cross an artificial bridge, with a pond underneath it, with some goldfish swimming around.

As we sat down the waiter asked if we would like the set menu or the lunch time buffet.

I turned to Nadine and asked her what she would like.

'Oh, let's have the menu please, my treat.'

The waiter came back with the menu and at the same time poured us both a glass of iced water. I took advantage of the water to take my tablets; the water was cold, bloody cold.

'Well, what are you having?' I asked Nadine.

'I will start with chicken and sweet corn soup, followed by chicken chop suey and fried rice. What do you fancy?'

'Well, I would like the same soup, I hope it is hot. So I will start with the same as you, but I will have the curried chicken with boiled rice. Would you have a glass of wine with me if I order a bottle?'

'That would be nice,' Nadine said. 'But I will just have the one glass, don't forget I am driving.'

'Good, then I will order a half bottle of white wine to go with the chicken.'

We drank a toast to our friendship and good health to each other.

The meal was excellent and now I had the taste for a drink.

'Nadine, would you mind if I stopped off to have a few drinks with Joe and his pals?'

'Not at all, while you are there I will see to some business at the bank.

'Speaking of which. How much do I owe you?'

'What for!' she exclaimed.

'What for? The accommodation and food, etc.', I said.

'I hope you are joking with me,' she replied.

'No, I wasn't. I always like to pay my own way.'

'Well you can forget it, this time it is on me.'

'Thank you very much, that's very generous of you.'

'You're welcome.'

With that sorted out we left the restaurant and got into the car.

The drive went just as quickly on the way back and Nadine dropped me at the Arc-en-Ciel.

As I walked in Joe called with a roar, 'You are back, what will you have to drink?'

'Do they have Bacardi rum here?'

'I will ask,' said Joe. He called the barman.

'Have you a Bacardi rum for my limey friend?'

'Yes we do,' he replied. 'What would he like with it?'

'I would like it in a tall glass with ice and filled with coke, please.'

As I have mentioned before, I am not the best drinker in the world. So six rums later I was talking broken biscuits.

'Right Joe, I have enjoyed this afternoon. I must get back and see Nadine.'

'Oh, you are frightened of her then?'

'No, but I have had enough to drink for now. I had best get some sleep as I am tired now.'

Walking back to the motel I certainly didn't feel the cold this time.

I walked into the motel with a big grin on my face like a Cheshire cat.

Nadine looked at me and smiled.

'You look very pleased with yourself, and I bet you are feeling no pain.'

'I think the expression, "feeling no pain" means, you are pissed.'

'Yes.'

'I have had a few drinks with Joe and his friends, and I have enjoyed them very much. But now I would like to go to your place and sleep it off. That's if it is all right by you.' I added, 'Ma chérie.'

'Mon chéri!' Nadine repeated. 'I was told you Englishmen were not romantic, but I know better now, especially after the last month or so. Go and wait in the car then. I will not be long, and I know when someone is buttering me up'

I kissed her on the cheek.

'If you think that will get you anywhere, you are right,' she smiled.

I walked to the car giggling. Nadine followed me about two minutes later.

'I am pleased you have had a nice time.'

'Thank you, Nadine, I have, but I am so tired now, I must have some sleep and rest.'

Needless to say, I slept all night.

Next morning it was Nadine's turn to wake me with a kiss.

'Bonjour, you slept good did you not?'

'I certainly did,' I replied, and I feel pretty good. I am ready for one of your big breakfasts.'

'There is plenty of time. Let's stay in bed for a while.'

'Oh no! Here we go again.' I grinned.

'You were grinning like that when you came back from the Arc-en-Ciel yesterday, and now I will wipe the grin off your face.'

'What on earth can you do, to do that?'

'Well for a start.' Nadine grabbed me by my hair and kissed me on the lips.

When she had finished I said, 'Oh no! Please have mercy, not that terrible ordeal.'

'Yes,' she laughed, 'you deserve all you get.'

'Okay, if that's the price I will have to pay, so be it.'

It was as good as all the other times; the chemistry between us seemed to match perfectly.

'Well, that's the first time I have paid the bill before I got the meal.'

'You have paid in full. What would you like for your breakfast?'

'A full English, please.'

We had a shower together, and we damn well nearly started again.

'Hold on,' I said. 'I have not been paid for the last one. I do not usually give credit.'

The both of us could always see the funny side and started laughing. Nadine gave a giggle and stepped out of the shower, not saying a word.

I felt like any other morning after being on the ale, bloody hungry. I stayed in the shower for ten more minutes, the hot water running down my body felt really good.

I sat at the table in my bath robe. There was orange juice and cereal already waiting for me.

'Nadine,' I shouted through, 'come and join me, please.'

Nadine came into the dining room with a big tray of food.

'There you go, help yourself.'

'Wow, that's what I call a breakfast.'

On the tray were fried eggs, bacon, sausage, tomatoes

and home fries. These are boiled sliced potatoes, fried, and they taste really good.

I made a bit of a pig of myself.

'That's set me up for the day, thank you very much.'

'You are welcome. It was paid for.'

'How about paying for your supper now?' she said with a cheeky grin.

'Not on a full stomach, Nadine, perhaps later.

What time are you going into town?'

'About thirty minutes, will you be ready?'

'I can get ready in three minutes, never mind thirty.'

'What are you doing today?' Nadine asked.

'I must try and see Mike. I have not seen him for a couple of days. I don't even know where he is, so if you can drop me off at Joe's place, I will try and find out where he's got to.'

When I got to the garage Joe was on the front talking to a customer, so I waited until he had finished.

'Bonjour, Joe, how are things with you?'

'Bonjour, mon ami. Things are just fine, and you?'

'I am okay. What I have come for is to ask you about Mike. I have not seen him for two or three days, do you know where he is?'

'Oui. He returned to the cabin to collect some things and to secure it for the winter. He did not have time when he fetched you back. He should be back sometime today.

'Good, I will buy him some lunch. That's if he is back in time. If you see him before me would you tell him I will be at the motel helping Nadine?'

'Helping Nadine! That's what you limeys call it?'

'Behave yourself, you get worse by the day. Au revoir.'

I pottered about the motel doing odd chores. It helped

to pass the time, otherwise I think I would be at the Arc-en-Ciel with Joe again, drinking, and I really don't want to do that.

I was putting some laundry away in a cupboard when the front desk bell rang. I was nearest so I went through. Who was standing there but big Mike.

Before he could say anything, I shouted to Nadine, 'Do you take big scruffy bears in this motel?'

'Certainly not. Why, is there one there?'

'Yes,' I said, 'and it is an ugly one at that.'

Mike laughed at that, and then we shook hands.

'Have you been I asked? I have missed you.'

'Well,' he said with a big sigh. 'I had to go back and tidy up after you.'

I smiled at that and asked Mike, 'Are you hungry?'

'What do you think? I have been on that skidoo for four hours.'

'Good, then I will buy you lunch at the Arc-en-Ciel.'

'Give me fifteen minutes to shower and change,' he said, 'and I will call back here for you.'

As Mike walked out the front door, Nadine came through from the back.

'I suppose you will be sleeping your lunch off again tonight.'

'No, I will not. I have had enough drink for the next few days. Besides I want to spend the evening with you'

'That very nice of you, I would like that myself.'

'Okay. What time will you be finished here?'

Nadine thought for a second or two.

'I have some business, and some bookwork to do here, so let's say about five thirty.'

'That will suit me fine, I can have a long talk with Mike over lunch. We have to sort a few things out ourselves; I will wait here in reception, okay?

'Right,' she said, 'I will see you then.' She then kissed me; it was one of her specials.

'You get yourself back in that office and get some work done, and leave us young lads alone.'

I was reading a magazine when the door opened.

'Come on,' he said. 'Hurry up, I'm starving.'

'That makes a change, you must let me know when you are not. And you look half human now you have cleaned up.'

'Come on, feed me,' he said, showing his big white teeth when we came out of the motel door.

There was a shout from across the street.

'Hey you two, don't go without me.' It was Joe.

I shouted back. 'Joe, we are going for a meal, we are not going drinking. We will see you later.'

'Okay, I suppose so,' he moaned.

I just shook my head and smiled.

Mike gave a chuckle and said, 'He loves his drink.'

While Mike and I had lunch we talked of what we were going to do.

'Well,' he said. 'I am going back to St John on Sunday. What are you doing?'

'I should come with you.'

'Do you think you can drive my four wheeler back for me? Or would you rather drive the car I came up in? That's if you decide to come, of course.'

'I would rather drive the car, if you do not mind, and yes, I will come. Let's make arrangements tomorrow.'

We finished our meal. I paid the bill, then asked Mike what was he planning on doing now?

'I will stay and have a few beers here. Do you want to stay and have some, Joe will be in shortly?'

'No, thank you. I am spending the evening with Nadine. I had enough yesterday. See you tomorrow.'

Walking back to the motel I bumped into Joe.

'Hi limey, come and have a drink with me.'

'No, thank you, Joe. Big Mike is in there, he will have a few with you. I am five minutes late already.'

'Five minutes late in this town is early,' he laughed.

I will not even try to figure that one out.

Nadine was just putting some ledgers in the motel safe when I walked in.

'That is good timing,' she said. 'I have just this minute finished. Are you ready to go now?'

'Yes,' I replied. 'You look surprised.'

'I am. I thought once you got with Mike and Joe that would be it for the day.'

'Well, if it was up to Joe it would have been.

What do you have planned for us?'

'I thought we would do what we did the other night.'

'Have a nice dinner, then watch some TV and have a drink of wine? Okay, that will do me nicely. A quiet night in with you suits me down to the ground.'

We drove away from the motel at six o'clock.

The house was lovely to walk into, warm, clean and welcoming.

'Can I help with the dinner?' I asked Nadine.

'Certainly, you can peel some potatoes while I have a shower. We can eat later.'

'I think I should help you with a shower, and then peel some potatoes.'

'Do as you are told. Peel some potatoes for me please. You can wait till later for the other.'

'What? Do you mean give you a shower later?' I said, with a cheeky grin. 'Just kidding, just kidding. Is that all you want me to do for now?'

'Yes. For now.'

I finished peeling the spuds, so I set the table and put some fancy napkins by the plates.

Nadine came through, looking as lovely as ever.

'Well,' she said. 'You have done this sort of thing before.'

'Yes, I have been on my own for some time now. Working and living by myself. One learns how to cook and look after oneself.'

'Good for you.' She smiled.

After dinner and the wine, I started to do my party trick. I was dozing off.

'Come on, let's get you into bed. You can have a good night's sleep.'

'You say that now,' I said to her. 'But I think...'

Nadine put her hand over my mouth. 'If you are going to complain, you can always stay here on the chesterfield.'

'No, I have no complaints, I was just teasing.

I think an awful lot of you. You are one of the nicest women I have ever met.'

'I bet you say that to all the girls.'

'No, I don't actually. I am quite fussy who I associate with.'

'You really mean that don't you?' she said.

'Yes, let's go to bed before you get carried away.'

We climbed the stairs, not saying a word.

I slept very deeply for a good five hours. When I awoke, it felt so good being here with Nadine; warm and comfortable just like I had dreamt about when I was out in the wilds. I put my arm around her and pulled her closer.

She stirred a little.

'Are you awake?' I whispered.

'No, not really. Can you not sleep?' she murmured.

'I have had a wonderful sleep, thank you.'

'Oh,' she said, 'if you can't sleep, no one sleeps, eh?'

I pulled her round and kissed her, this was one of my specials.

'Wow, you are really better now. That was great.'

We made love, had our shower, got back into bed and went off to sleep again.

At breakfast next morning I said to Nadine,

'Mike and I have decided to go back on Sunday.'

Nadine's face physically dropped and tears came to her eyes.

'I am sorry if you're upset about that. I would not hurt you for the world.'

'I was just a bit shocked. It seems so sudden, but I knew it would have to happen.'

'Listen, Nadine,' I said, taking her in my arms. 'I have some things I have to take care of back home so I have to leave shortly. I have put them off for too long now, although I would like to stay here with you, but they must be sorted soon.'

'Yes, I know,' she said tearfully.

'Nadine, it has been wonderful, I don't want this to end. Don't worry I will be back. Let me get things in order back home and I will return. Of course I will phone you two or three times a week at least.'

Nadine's face lit up.

'That's better,' I said.

'Will you really come back, or are you just saying that to make me feel better?'

'Yes, I really mean it; I will be back in the spring. Now let's enjoy the little time we have left together.'

'Okay,' she said. 'What are your plans?'

'Well, I am having the party on Friday night, then Mike and I are setting off early Sunday morning, so we can spend all Saturday and Saturday night together. Mike said we can get back in a day, but I might not be up to it, I will have to wait and see.

'Talking of Mike, would you mind if I borrowed your car. I want to go and see him and ask if the roads are clear enough to do the trip in a day, and also if this nice weather is going to hold.'

'May I come into town with you?' Nadine asked. 'I want to spend all the time you have left here together.'

'Yes, of course, I was not thinking.'

'What's new about men?'

'Now we will have less sarcasm, if you don't mind. Come on then let's go.'

Mike was just coming out of the motel as we drew up.

'Just the man I want to see.'

Mike looked at me a bit puzzled.

'Oh, don't worry,' I said, 'there is nothing wrong. I would like a little chat with you about getting back to St John.'

'We are still going on Sunday morning?' Mike asked.

'Yes, that's what I want to talk to you about. Why are we doing it in one day?'

'Once I set off I do not like stopping,' said Mike.

'Do you think we can do it in a day?'

'If no more snow falls between now and Sunday, yes,' he said. 'Why do you ask?'

'Well, I needed to stop a couple of times on the way out here. It took me more than a day.'

'Right,' he said a little impatiently. 'Which way did you come?'

After I described my route here and showed him on the map, he explained, 'That's where you went wrong. I know a few short cuts, It will be early Monday morning when we arrive, say one thirty to two o'clock, but we can do it in one go.'

'Okay, I will try it your way, but I can tell you now it's going to be bloody hard for me, but I will try. I will let you know if anything is going wrong.'

'Good.' He smiled. 'What should we do today?'

'I can spend a couple of hours with you if you like, but, and I mean but, I will not be drinking. I don't care what you or Joe says my next drink will be at the party on Friday night.'

'Come on you big girl, let's go and see Joe,' he replied.

'Just hang on, I will tell Nadine what's what. By the way,' I asked, 'what day is it today?'

'The cold must have got to your head. It's Thursday,' he replied.

'Then the party is tomorrow night. I must talk to Nadine and make some arrangements.'

Big Mike shrugged his shoulders. 'Okay, I will be over at Joe's place. Come over there when you are ready.'

When I went back into the motel, Nadine was in her office. I rang the bell and she looked up.

'Come in. You were quick. I thought you would be spending some time with Mike.'

'Later,' I said. 'First things first. It's the party tomorrow night and I have not made any arrangements, I would like your help, please.'

'Certainly,' she said with glee.

Nadine looked quite pleased about being able to help.

'What would you suggest?' I asked.

'Do you want a sit down meal? That will be very expensive, or would you like a buffet?'

'I think I will have the sit down meal, after all this a special occasion.'

'Okay, let me sort things out here, and I will go and talk to the manager of the Arc-en-Ciel. We can work something out I am sure.'

'I kissed her cheek once again, 'Merci ma chérie. How can I ever thank you?'

'I will think of something.'

'I bet.'

I spent the rest of the day with Joe and Mike, and no, I didn't touch a drop of alcohol, not even that evening back at Nadine's.

Next morning at breakfast I asked Nadine about the arrangements for tonight.

'Is everything arranged?'

'Well,' she said. 'I spoke to the manager and he is going

to put on a special menu for you. Each full meal that is ordered will cost $20. I hope that is all right with you.'

'Yes,' I replied. 'And that seems quite reasonable to me. After all they do very good meals. What time would he like us to be there?'

'He would like us all to be sat down at or before nine thirty.'

'Therefore, I think it would be a good idea if we could get there for seven thirty. That will give us a chance to have a drink or two before eating. What do you say?'

'Yes, why not, we should make a night of it. After all I don't know when, or indeed if, we will dine together again.'

'Don't start to get melancholy on me already.

I will come with you to the motel and phone everyone from there. That's if you don't mind?'

'Not at all, I will help you,' Nadine replied.

'Good, let's make tracks.'

'Back at the motel I phoned the hospital and asked the receptionist to tell whoever wanted to, to come to the party tonight at the Arc-en-Ciel, they would be very welcome.

Nadine phoned Joe and asked him and his apprentice if they would like to come. Needless to say, Joe accepted.

I also asked Nadine to invite her employees.

'Okay, that is that then.'

I thanked Nadine the usual way.

'What are you going to do now?' she asked.

'I thought I would potter about the motel, and do some work for you. Are there any odd jobs you want doing?'

'I'm glad you asked,' she said with a wry smile, and with that she pulled out a list.

'Me and my big mouth.'

'Do you want to do them or not?' The smile had gone.

'Nadine, where has your sense of humour gone? I was only kidding.'

A broad smile spread across her face. As one did on mine.

We both laughed like always.

The day went fast and I enjoyed fixing things, it occupied my mind and I didn't even stop for lunch. I just had coffee with a hot dog that Nadine had brought in.

Nadine and I finished at the motel around 3.30 p.m. and went back to her place.

'Would you like anything to eat?' she asked me.

'No thank you, I don't want to spoil my dinner tonight, but I have something else in mind.'

'What would that be?'

'Well, first I would like us to have a jacuzzi together, after which, we could have a couple of hours in bed.'

'You are tired after a bit of work?'

'No, I was thinking of something else, as I said.'

'Okay. What would the "something else" be?'

'That's a surprise!' I said, with a silly look.

'I like surprises,' she said.

'You will like this surprise.'

We laughed for five minutes while we undressed, before getting into the jacuzzi.

After making love, we spent a couple of hours resting. I slept well which was new.

I made love to Nadine once more before getting out of bed and having a shower and getting dressed into some decent clothes.

Nadine started to get ready after me, but just like a

women it took a little longer for her. Having said that, it was well worth the wait, she looked stunning.

'You look good enough to eat,' I said to her.

'We are going to dinner now, you can have me for dessert later.'

'Okay, let's eat now.' I grinned.

'Get out of here!'

I think that means, scram.

'Nadine, let's get a taxi, so you can have a drink as well.'

'I intended to, you do not think I would let you get drunk without me again do you?'

'How long will you be?' I asked.

'What is your hurry? There is plenty of time. I am just about ready now, two minutes.'

'Good. I hate waiting.'

'I have noticed,' she replied.

'Besides, I have a surprise for you,' I said with a glint in my eye.

'Another one? I know your surprises.'

'Not this one. This is a big surprise.'

Needless to say, her two minutes turned into thirty.

We arrived at the Arc-en-Ciel at seven fifteen. Joe and his help were already there. Mike was right behind us, and two of the nurses had turned up.

'Right you lot, what would you like to drink? Before you answer I'm ordering a couple of bottles of chardonnay, so if you would like to share it with me you are quite welcome.'

Most nodded in agreement.

'Okay, two bottles please and seven glasses.'

Well that was the start.

About eight thirty the doctor and two more nurses came

in. This made me feel good, I can now repay back a little of what they have done for me. I ordered four more bottles of wine as it seemed to be going down well with everyone.

The night went very well and everyone enjoyed themselves. I took it easy on the wine, but I made a bit of a pig of myself when it came to the meal, which was wonderful.

After we had finished the starters, I stood up and asked for some attention.

'Ladies and gentleman, I have an announcement to make.'

I turned to Nadine, asked her to stand, then handed her a small box.

'Would you please accept this from me?' Before placing the box in her hand I said, 'I hope you will.'

'What is it?' she asked.

'Open it and find out,' I said softly.

She opened the box very slowly. When the engagement ring was visible Nadine stopped in her tracks.

'Well?' I said. 'What is your answer? Are we engaged or not?'

Tears were falling down her cheeks now and her lips were moving but nothing was coming out of her mouth, she was speechless.

The room was in silence with everyone waiting for the answer.

It must have been two minutes or more before she pulled herself together enough to give me her answer.

'Yes. We are.'

The room exploded with applause, clapping and cheering.

Nadine put her arms around my neck and whispered, 'You have made me very happy. Yes, again I accept.'

The party and the night went far too fast. It is always the same, when you are having a good time, it just flies by. Just the opposite to being stranded in two feet of snow with no food.

Nadine woke me next morning with a cup of coffee.

'Morning, sleepy head, what would you like to do today?'

'Well,' I yawned, 'I think that you should choose, after all it's your town. You tell me.'

'Okay,' she said. 'Seeing as it's our last day I would love to go for a long drive this morning.

Have lunch somewhere nice, and then spend the rest of the day at home making love to you.'

'Go on then, you have talked me into it, you smoothy. That sounds wonderful. I will be with you in ten minutes.'

We left the house at nine fifteen, driving along the main road out of town. I felt a little saddened, knowing that this will be my last time for a while that we will be driving down this road.

Nadine drove for about one and a half hours, it was approaching eleven o'clock and we had hardly spoken a word.

Then Nadine said, 'Shall we have lunch early; that's if you feel like some?'

'Go on then, I could manage a burger and French fries with a nice cup of tea.'

'You certainly like your tea, but I was thinking of something really nice for our last lunch.'

'Yes of course, we will do what you want. It's your day.'

Nadine chooses a semi-classy restaurant for lunch. We took about forty minutes over our meal, and again we didn't say much. I suppose we both thought the day would last longer, knowing it was our last one. For a while anyway.

'Right,' I said, 'that's the meal finished with. Let me think, what was the next thing you suggested?'

A big smile came on Nadine's face.

'Oh, that's right. You have to go to work. Come on, let's get you there then.'

'No,' Nadine said. 'I have arranged for the whole day off, just to spend it with you.'

We had our little giggle.

'Nadine, would you let me drive back please? I have to get used to it for, dare I say, tomorrow?'

'Yes, you can drive back, but you can't say the other.'

The drive back always passes quicker, why is this?

I drove to Joe's garage to say goodbye and thanks again; he was there with his head under the bonnet of a truck.

'Joe, I have come to say farewell to you, I am leaving in the morning with Mike.'

'Yes, I know, Mike has told me. I hope it will not be long before you are back.'

'Thank you for everything, and I hope it will not be long either.'

He wiped his hands and shook mine with one and with the other put it around me and gave me a hug. I was not used to a man hugging me. I was brought up to think it was only sissies who did that sort of thing, but I have noticed over here and in the States it seemed common practice.

'Behave yourself,' I said, a little embarrassed. I made a joke of it. 'You will have Nadine getting jealous,' I laughed.

'Will you not have one more drink with me before you leave?' Joe asked.

I looked at Nadine.

'Go on,' she said, 'I will join you. Let's go to the Arc-en-Ciel and I will treat you both.'

'Okay, but first I must get hold of Mike,'

Joe interrupted. He has just gone back to the motel. I will ring him and he can meet us at the bar.'

Joe made the call, then the three of us walked to the Arc-en-Ciel.

I suggested a bottle of my favourite wine. That would do all four of us and that way I would not drink too much.

The bottle was no sooner opened when Mike walked in.

'That is good timing,' Joe said to him.

I poured the wine.

'May I propose a toast to all four of us, our friendship and long may it last.'

As I drank to the toast I put my arm around Nadine's waist and pulled her closer to me.

I had two classes of wine, then told Mike and Joe that Nadine and I had other things to do before I leave in the morning.

They both started to giggle like a couple of kids.

'For two big men, you can be very childish,' I said with a big smile.

Mike said, 'Take the car. Here are the keys. It's outside Joe's. I will be outside Nadine's place in the morning, eight o'clock sharp.'

'I will be ready Mike, see you then.'

I shook hands once again with Joe, then Nadine and I left.

I picked up the car and drove behind Nadine to her house. Once inside I started to pack; it did not take long, or that's how it seemed. Not too much was said.

'Now woman, what was your next suggestion?' I roared.

'Stop trying to act like a man,' she retorted. 'I would like us to have a jacuzzi and relax for a while. Come on. Last one in is a stinky bum.'

We both ran towards the jacuzzi grabbing hold of each other to stop one of us getting there first, like two kids in a race to the end of the street.

The jacuzzi was on full power, and so was Nadine. After getting out of the jacuzzi we lay on the bed for a little while; it did not take long before we were making love again.

We dozed off for a good couple of hours, we awoke about seven thirty, and yes, we made love again.

'Right. I would like something to eat now, please. Not too much because I have to get an early night ready for tomorrow.'

'Okay,' Nadine said. 'I will fix you up a meal.'

'Nothing too fancy.' I said. 'Perhaps an omelette or something.'

Sitting at the table we just kept looking at each other, not saying a word.

'Let's have a drink of wine,' Nadine suggested, 'just for you and me.'

'Go on, make it just one, then I will have to have that early night.'

We did not quite finish the bottle.

Once in bed, it did not take me long to get off to sleep.

I woke up in the early hours wanting to go to the toilet,

or washroom as they call it over here. Nadine was not in the bed with me, I was a little surprised.

I had my wee and went downstairs. Nadine was sat there on the chesterfield.

'What on earth are you doing down here on your own?' I asked.

'Oh, I was a bit restless and I did not want to spoil your night's sleep so I got up.'

I could tell that she had been crying.

'Nadine, please do not cry. We have had a wonderful time together and we should be thankful for that. You will only spoil it by crying and make me feel bad about going.'

'Yes, you are right again.'

'Again?' I replied. 'When was the first time?'

That brought a smile to her face.

'How about one of us ravishing the other?' I said.

'Well, should we toss a coin, or see who does it first?'

'Let's see who is first.'

With that we ran back to the bedroom. I cannot remember who ravished who, but who cares? It was very enjoyable to say the least.

It was six o'clock next morning when I got up, had a shower and went down for my breakfast.

Nadine asked, 'What do you want for breakfast?'

'I would like the works, please, I think I am going to need it. I have a long day ahead.'

I lifted up her hair and I kissed her on the side of her neck.

'Bonjour, did you sleep good for the last few hours?'

'No wonder, look what you put me through.'

'What I put you through? I thought it was you who ravished me.'

'Get away with you, I am not that sort of man.'

We put our arms around each other and laughed.

While Nadine made the breakfast I put my bags into the car, ready for the off. When I came back in the food was on the table.

'That looks as good as ever, and before we go any further I do not want any crying from you. It will only spoil my day, and I know you do not want to do that, do you?'

'I will try my best, but I can't promise,' came the reply.

'No, that's not good enough,' I said sternly. 'I want no crying at all, you must wait until I have gone. Is it a deal?'

'Okay, it's a deal,' she said' smiling.

'Good, let's eat.'

When we had finished breakfast I asked Nadine to walk me to the car, this she did.

'Well,' I said, taking her in my arms. 'I am sorry to be leaving, but at the same time glad that we are engaged. That way I have something to come back for. You will wait for me, yes?'

'Of course,' she said tearfully.

'No crying, that's the deal.'

Mike beeped his horn, and shouted, 'Come on, put the woman down. Let's get some miles in.'

I thought it's all right you shouting, but I did not want to let go.

Nadine and I kissed for a long time, not wanting to stop, because we both knew that when we did it would be the last for a while.

'Right, Mike, I will be with you in one minute.'

'Au revoir ma chérie.' It took all my willpower to let her go.

I waved to Mike as I walked to the car.

'Okay, let's go.' I turned the key and the engine fired into life. As I drove off down that lovely drive I looked back once more, Nadine was waving with both arms.

I just followed Mike. I didn't even remember looking left, right or any other direction. If Mike turned, I turned. If Mike braked, I braked. I was on remote. All I could think of was Nadine, I do not know if we went fast, slow or whatever, it did not matter too much to me.

Next thing I know, Mike is pulling into a roadside cafe. I pulled up behind him, and Mike came over to my window and knocked.

'Hi buddy, I am having something to eat, how about you?'

'No thanks, Mike, I am not hungry at the moment. How long have we been going?'

'Two and a half hours.'

'Hell, that went quick. I will get my head down in the back seat if you do not mind. Give me a shake when you are ready to set off again.'

'Okay,' he said. 'Are you all right?'

'Yes, just a little tired.'

Mike woke me about forty minutes later.

'How do you feel now?'

'Just great. I needed that kip.'

'I got two hot dogs and a cup of coffee for you. You can eat and drink while you drive.'

'Good man, I can eat something now.'

We got on the way. I felt a little better for the rest, and

the food and drink went down well. I was a lot hungrier than I realised.

It was the same routine. I just followed Mike. I was still in a daze. Next time we stopped we were at the ferry ready for crossing.

'Mike, I can't go much further. I am going to spend the night in Rivière-du-Loup. I will catch up with you sometime tomorrow evening in St John.'

'Okay buddy, if you do not feel up to it, I don't blame you. I can take you to a nice motel for the night and see you settled in.

It didn't take long to find the motel, I am pleased to say. I was aching all over, there was no way I could get to St John in one go.

After booking in Mike said, 'Take it easy, we will have a drink tomorrow night. See you then.'

'Okay, Mike,' I replied. 'You take it easy on those roads. Bye big fellow.'

Mike roared off as if there was no tomorrow, he obviously liked driving fast. I was too tired to even have a shower I just got into to bed and closed my eyes.

Well that was one of the best night's sleep I have ever had, I didn't know where I was when I woke up. I only know that Nadine was not with me; talking of that I will give her a call.

The phone had no sooner rang when Nadine answered it.

'That was quick,' I said. 'Is that you, ma chérie?'

'Oh am I glad to hear your voice. I have missed you very much. Are you okay?'

'Yes and no.'

'Before I could say another word she said,

'What is wrong?'

'Don't worry, I am all right. I have stopped at Rivière-du-Loup, I could not go any further last night. I was too tired to carry on. I booked into a motel and big Mike went on to St John.'

Nadine sobbed, 'I wish you were back with me.'

'It will not be long,' I said, hoping it would settle her down. But there was not much chance of that at the moment.

We talked for quite a long time and we both did not want to stop.

'This will be costing you a lot of money,' she said. 'Next time make it a collect call.'

'Well I must get on my way, Nadine or I will be spending another night here, au revoir.'

We were like those two kids again, she would not put the phone down and neither would I.

'Okay, that's it. I am hanging up now, bye.'

It took all my willpower to actually put the phone down.

I had a long hot shower and it brought me back to life. I was ready for the last part of the journey. I had a quick breakfast, filled up the car and got on the road.

I was more aware of driving now, reading the signs and watching the road, which is always a good idea, it's safer that way.

Passing through Grand Falls I thought, not this time but sometime soon. I arrived in St John at four o'clock, very exhausted. I had only stopped once for a snack and a wee.

I booked into the County hotel. I had spent a weekend when I first arrived. It was in the centre of the town and very good for the price.

The first think I did was to give Mike a ring.

'Hi, buddy, you made it then?'

'Only just Mike,' I said. 'I found it very hard, but I am here now safe and sound.'

'Where are you?'

'I have booked in at the County hotel down town.'

'When you have settled in come down to George's tavern around eight tonight, and I will buy you a beer.'

'Not tonight, Mike, thank you. I am far too knackered for that or anything else. Let's make it tomorrow night.'

'Okay buddy, I will see you then.'

I lay on the bed to rest; the next thing I know it's eight thirty. I am hungry, stiff and still aching from the driving. Pulling myself up, brushing myself down, I went out for a walk and something to eat. A burger or hot dog will do just fine, with a can of coke; that will get me through till breakfast. Walking into the night air, it felt very cold and crisp.

On my return, I undressed, had a shower and then phoned Nadine.

'Bonsoir, Nadine. How are you feeling tonight?'

'A whole lot better for you calling me. Where are you now?'

'I am back in St John, staying in the County hotel Would you like the phone number?'

'Yes please,' she quickly said.

We talked for almost thirty minutes before saying good night to each other, after which I was ready for bed again. I was beginning to think I will never be fully fit again.

I feel so tired, I intend to stay in bed all night and most of tomorrow. So I'd better put the "Do Not Disturb" notice on the door handle, otherwise the housemaid will be knocking on the bloody door in the morning.

Waking up at seven next morning, I lay for a while and then got up and made myself a cup of coffee. I sat on the side of the bed looking out of the window at the traffic going by. I suppose they were going to work. I was very glad I was not going to work. I could not handle that at the present time.

Finishing the coffee and the complimentary biscuit they put in the room I used the washroom then I climbed back into bed.

The phone woke me. I reached over and answered, 'Hello, who is it, please?'

'It's I, mon chéri.'

'Oh, good morning, Nadine. Nice to hear from you again.'

'Morning? It's twenty-five after twelve.'

Christ I must have needed that.

'Are you still in bed?' she asked.

'Yes, and I have enjoyed the sleep. Are things all right with you?'

'Yes thanks, I am at the motel, working.'

'I was thinking of work at seven this morning. Just thinking of it must have made me tired.'

Nadine giggled at that.

'What are your plans for today?'

'Well,' I said, 'I will walk into town, have some lunch then go to the travel agents to book a flight home.'

There was no answer for a while.

'Are you still there?' I asked.

'Oui, I wish you were booking a trip back here.'

'Yes I know, but as I said, I have some business to take care of and see my family at the same time.'

I could feel Nadine was taking this part badly. I did not want that so I said a quick goodbye and hung up before she started to cry.

After hanging up I did not waste any time getting ready. I was soon walking down the road to the town centre. After having a big meal I wandered over to Cain's travel and booked the flight.

I was to fly out of St John the following evening.

The flight was from St John to Montreal and onto Manchester the following day, landing at eight thirty Thursday morning.

After booking my flight I walked around the town centre aimlessly, the flight home could not come quick enough now.

I was lonelier here in the city, than I was out at the cabin. At least at the cabin I could talk to Fatso and friend, not to mention Rocky Racoon.

I will have to wait till tonight before I have anyone to converse with. I was thinking a lot about Nadine while I walked. That's it, I will get a taxi back to the hotel and give her a call. That will buck me up; I never did explain that expression to her.

After the call I slept till six forty–five. I then packed my bags with all the stuff I knew I would not need until I got home; it will save time tomorrow. I do not know why I need to save time as I will have all day to get ready. I then got changed for my night out with big Mike, but first I must eat as I do not want to drink on an empty stomach.

When I got to George's tavern on Germain Street there

were already a few people in there enjoying themselves. Most looked like they had just come straight from work. I recognised a few faces from the oil refinery that I had worked on.

'Hi buddy, over here, I have saved you a seat. Sit down, I will get us some beers.'

When Mike came back he introduced the men sat around the table, to me. I really enjoyed being with someone. It was not just the company, it was because they all seemed to be having a good time and it made me forget about things that had gone on.

Halfway through the night a friend of Mike's came over to the table to say hello. He was a big Norwegian I had worked with on the oil refinery.

'Where have you been?' he said to Mike. 'I have not seen you for a week or two.'

'Out at the cabin,' Mike explained. At that point Mike turned and said to me, 'You know Peter Larson do you?'

'Yes, I have worked with him.'

Peter said to me, 'Yes, I do know you, but you look different.'

'Yes, I have been on a diet.'

Mike had just taken a big swig of his beer. I thought I was going to get the lot all over me.

Peter shook my hand. He said, 'I will talk to you later, nice seeing you again.'

'Christ, Mike, I thought you were big but he takes the cake. How big is he?'

'Six seven and a lot heavier than me. Have you seen the advert, "Drink Canada Dry"?'

'Yes,' I answered.

'Well he nearly has.'

That made for a light relief.

'By the way, when are you going home?' Mike asked me.

'I fly out tomorrow night, via Montreal.

'I will give you a run to the airport if you like. What time should I pick you up?'

'Well I have to check out of the hotel at eleven. Would you pick me up at say half past?'

'No problem, it's the least I can do.'

'I think you have done enough for me already, I can never thank you.'

'Don't start that again.'

'I must have had six or seven beers before I left and I enjoyed them. I was feeling okay but I have had enough now.

'Right, Mike, I have enjoyed that. I am going to walk back to my hotel now.'

'Have another beer.'

'No thanks, that's my lot. I am off back to bed. See you in the morning. Good night.'

Once outside I turned left and went down Germain onto King Street East, took a right up to Crown Street, hung a left again, as they say over here, onto the hotel. It was further than I realised I wish I had taken a taxi now.

Was I glad to get in. Once inside I did my usual party trick and hung my clothes on the floor and flopped into bed.

Next morning I was up bright and early, packed the rest of my things and went down to the restaurant and had a big breakfast. Now I was ready for the day,

Sure enough, Mike was on time.

'How are you this fine morning? Throw your stuff in the back and let's go.'

'Mike, just take it easy, there is no hurry. There's all today untouched, let me enjoy the ride to the airport.'

'Okay,' he said reluctantly.

Much to my surprise he did take it nice and slow.

Once at the airport I took my bags out of his truck and said, 'Mike, you do not have to come in with me, let's say goodbye here.'

' Okay, I have to get back anyway.'

'Mike, a great many thanks again. I will give you a call when I land.'

'It was a pleasure. You look after yourself and get some decent meals in you and build yourself up.'

We shook hands for a long time. This time it was me who hugged Mike.

'Thanks, buddy. I will never forget what you did for me.'

I walked to the terminal with my bags, turned and waved. Mike waved back, got into his truck and roared off. I just shook my head. There he goes again, the crazy Canadian. Like a bat out of hell. I would not say that to his face.

I hung around the airport for what seemed a week. Like I said earlier, I just want to get home now, the sooner the better.

The flight to Montreal was a good one. Once there I gave Nadine a call. We did not have a lot to say. Why was that? I do not know, you tell me.

I boarded my flight and got a window seat, not that I cared. We took off on time, thank goodness for that. I hate sitting on the plane and getting nowhere, it bores the arse off me.

I settled in, had a meal and put a blanket around me ready to watch the film.

'Excuse me,' I said to the stewardess, 'what is the film tonight?'

'It's called *Jeremiah Johnson*.'

'Oh yes, and what is it about please?'

'It's about a young man who is fed up with city life. He gets himself a couple of horses and goes up into the wilderness of Canada. He gets attacked by a bear and nearly freezes to death.' She stopped. 'I will not tell you anymore, I do not want to spoil it for you. Why are you grinning?'

'Oh, it's nothing. I did not mean to be rude, but I think I will give this film a miss, thank you.'

The End